BRING ME
the HEAD
of YORKIE
GOODMAN

Advance praise for Bring Me the Head of Yorkie Goodman

"Bill Wallace, the protagonist of *Bring Me the Head of Yorkie Goodman*, learns you *can* go home again but that it's probably not a good idea if you're also accompanied by a psychotic enforcer named Carp with more than one hidden agenda. Giving Peckinpah a smile, Tarantino a wink, and McCarthy a nod, Yates puts Wallace in the fast lane to hell and Seymour, Indiana. Crime fiction aficionados will not want to miss catching a ride."

–Lynn Kostoff, author of *Words to Die For* and *A Choice of Nightmares*

Rowdy Yates writes with a style that plunges the reader into the world of the story, in this case a startlingly fun and fresh take on the well-worn crime novel. *Bring Me the Head of Yorkie Goodman* is sometimes comic, sometimes tragic, sometimes unclassifiable, always beautiful, never dull - like Warren Oates and Elmore Leonard walked onto the set of Fargo. And yet, underneath the suspense and the gunfire and the dreary dusk of the heartland, there's real heart here, real love for the places we call home and the people we'd do anything to protect.

—Matthew Fogarty, Editor of *Cartagena Journal* and Co-Editor of *Yemassee Journal*

Fast, bloody, and taut as razor-wire, *Bring Me the Head of Yorkie Goodman* roils with action and dark humor, plus the occasional moment of jaw-dropping poignancy. If you're a fan of Elmore Leonard, Cormac McCarthy, Samuel Beckett, or the Coen brothers, you need to add Jared Yates Sexton to your reading list.

—Michael Meyerhofer, author of *Wytchfire*

Bring Me the Head of Yorkie Goodman, with its liquor-slick voice and finely tuned prose, is 100% Hoosier grit. This is the debut of a serious—and seriously good—author of crime fiction. Bear witness. —Andrew Scott, author of *Naked Summer*

At the pounding heart of Yates's superb first novel are good men doing bad despite their conscience and bad men doing worse in the absence of their conscience, and every shade of moral corruption in between. More than anything, Yates knows these guys and these places the rest of us tend to avoid and brings the grittiest of language to bare their ink-black souls on the page. He gets inside these characters' heads and under their skin to bleed out the darkest heart of the human condition. By the end of *Bring Me the Head of Yorkie Goodman,* Yates has managed to do what the best novels of any genre should: implicate the conscience of nearly everyone involved, not the least of whom, you, my dear reader.

—Benjamin Drevlow, author of *Bend with the Knees and Other Love Advice from My Father*

BRING ME the HEAD of YORKIE GOODMAN

Rowdy Yates

NEW PULP PRESS
Published by New Pulp Press, LLC, 926 Truman Avenue,
Key West, Florida 33040, USA.

For information contact:
editor@newpulppress.com

ISBN-13: 978-0692387566 (New Pulp Press)
ISBN-10: 069238/560

For LB

"You might think you could run away and change your name and I don't know what all. Start over. And then one mornin' you wake up and look at the ceilin' and guess who's layin' there?"

—Cormac McCarthy, *No Country For Old Men*

Chapter 1

Here's what you have to understand, Boss said as he walked around Wallace and fell into the oversized leather chair behind his desk. It was covered in yellow legal pads, envelopes, crumpled up pieces of paper, a stack of folders, and the office, with its blinds all drawn, was nearly pitch black except for a lamp in the corner. Boss cracked his knuckles in the shadows and managed a smile. You run up debts, he said, and you can run from 'em for a while, hide here or hide there, but someday, down the road, they'll catch up with you.

I hear you, Wallace said.

Do you? Boss said.

I do. And I've always been grateful.

Then you don't hear me. We're not talking about you. We're not talking about you and me here.

Okay, Wallace said. I just wanted to put that out there.

Good, Boss said. I appreciate that, Wallace. I do. But we've got other business here.

What kind of business?

Debt-collecting business. Boss leaned back in his leather chair and kicked his feet up and onto the desk. He was a big man, easily three hundred pounds, and when his feet and round calves hit the top, it sounded like the desk might collapse. How you feel about going back home? he said.

To Indiana? Wallace said.

To Indiana.

I don't know. Lot of shit back there.

A whole mess of shit, Boss said. I'd say one of the biggest messes of shit.

That where I'm heading?

That'd be the place.

That's fine, Wallace said, shifting in his seat. I'll do it. Whatever you say, you got it, you know that, but I got to tell you it don't make me happy.

Didn't expect it would, Boss said, pulling a pack of Lucky Strikes out of his breast pocket and lighting up. He offered one to Wallace but Wallace shook him off. My hands are tied here, Boss said. There's a lot of shit back there for you, a lot of heat, but I need someone who knows the area. Someone who knows how these places work. When we picked up operations and headed East we lost a bunch of good people, you know that. Only people left who know that place are you and me and I can't head back that way.

Whatever you want, I'll do it, Wallace said. I owe you big for what you did for me.

We both know what I did, Boss said. That's not something we need to get into.

I'm just thankful. That's all.

Good. Just know this ain't me hanging some kind of debt over your head. It just makes sense is all.

Got it.

You'll leave tomorrow, early as possible, drive the twelve hours and set up outside of Seymour.

My old stomping grounds, Wallace said.

That's right. You're gonna have to take care of this situation. You and Carp.

Carp? Carp's going?

Carp's going.

Carp and I don't work too good together, Wallace said.

Carp don't work too good with anybody. Boss stubbed out his cigarette and picked a folder off the desk. He passed it over to Wallace. All the details are in there. Just stay out of Carp's way and he'll stay out of yours.

Has to be Carp?

Has to be.

Wallace opened the folder and looked at the first page. There was a picture of an older man wearing a Carhartt jacket, a John Deere hat. Looked like he was standing next to an old pickup. By the picture was written the name Yorkie Goodman and below that an address. Who's this guy? Wallace asked.

Just a guy.

Just a guy, Wallace said. Just a guy but you have to send Carp after him.

Don't go over thinking this thing. Drive out there with Carp, spend a couple days in the Hoosier state, and get the job done. Nothing more, nothing less.

No problem, Wallace said and got out of the chair and headed for the door. I'll see you when I get back, he said.

One thing, Boss said. I know what it's like to head back home. I've been there. It's nothing a guy can't understand. But when you get out there, you take mind not to go over any of your old tracks.

Okay, Wallace said.

You understand what I'm saying?

I understand what you're saying.

You get down in those hills, Boss said, and you might start thinking about looking up people you used to know in another life.

No, sir.

That starts happening, you think twice. Got me?

I got you, Wallace said.

I mean it, Boss said. This is business. This isn't a fucking family reunion.

Business, Wallace said.

Don't you forget, Boss said, you still got a lot of heat on you out there.

A lot of heat, Wallace said.

You leave well enough alone.

Don't worry about it, Boss. Tunnel-vision.

Tunnel-vision, Boss said.

Wallace opened the door to the office and let himself out. Some light from the other room leaked in and the office lit up for a second.

Boss was working another Lucky Strike out of his pack and sparking his lighter. Tunnel-vision, he said again.

Chapter 2

Wallace drove to the nearest drugstore and found the aisle with travel toiletries. He picked a foldable-toothbrush, a shaving kit, a stick of deodorant, and a thumb-sized bottle of shampoo. Before he left he saw a small first-aid kit and grabbed that too. At the register a woman in a red vest rang him up and smiled.

Going on a trip? she said.

Yes, ma'am, Wallace said. All the way out to Indiana.

Well, the woman said, that's exciting. I've never been out that way, but I hear good things. Got business out there?

Yes ma'am. Got business. The woman put his things into a bag and handed him his receipt. She told him to have a good trip, and he was about to walk out the automatic doors, but for some reason he turned to her again and had to add, I've got relations out there.

In his car he put the bag on the passenger-side floorboard and got the folder again. He looked over the first few pages. Yorkie Goodman was sixty-two years old, damn near Boss' age, and he had a farm just outside of Seymour. The people who'd written the report had their shit in a row. They knew everything there was to know about Yorkie. Where he'd gone to school, every illness he'd ever had, where he'd met his wife and when she'd died of breast cancer. In a nice neat paragraph they'd spelled out his daily routine:

5:30 - Wakes up, makes a pot of coffee

5:45-6:15 - Drinks coffee at kitchen table, reads newspaper and eats a breakfast of five sunny-side-up eggs and four pieces of bacon

6:15-14:30 - Works in field, repairs equipment, mills around farm

14:30-14:45 - Showers and dresses

14:45-16:00 - Drives into town to have lunch at Thompson's Family Diner, picks up supplies and groceries at the Sur-Way Supermarket, stops at In-And-Out Liquors for a six-pack of Busch Light beer

16:00-16:30 - Drinks two Busch Lights and watches television

16:30-17:00 - Calls son (Mike) on the telephone

17:00-20:00 - Drinks rest of Busch Lights and watches television

20:00-20:15 - Prepares for bed

20:15 - Retires

Wallace read it over a few times. Something didn't seem right. In that rigid schedule there didn't seem to be enough time to get into any trouble. When he'd first talked to Boss, it'd seemed like maybe this was a fella who ran meth in his free time or some other illegal business. It'd sounded strange from the beginning, but he had faith in Boss and figured it'd all be clear once he read the folder. He read it again just to make sure he wasn't missing anything. He wasn't. Yorkie Goodman seemed like just another old man.

From the store Wallace drove to a restaurant down the road a ways. It was a Mexican place called

Bueno Hermanas, his wife's favorite. The kids didn't care for it much, but it was Cindy he was worried about. She wasn't going to take his heading off too well and he wanted to try and blunt the blow. He sat down at the bar and got a beer. When the waitress came around, he ordered grilled *pollo* with rice and beans for himself and Cindy. For the kids he got a couple of hamburgers and fries.

While he waited, he drank his beer and watched the television behind the bar. The bartender was making a whole line of margaritas and pressing their rims into a bed of salt. It was busy, especially for a Wednesday night, and Wallace sat there and listened to the people around him.

On the television was a replay of the North Carolina game from the Saturday before. They were playing some small Division II school and beating the hell out of them. Wallace had seen the game when it first aired and couldn't believe how easy it all looked. North Carolina had moved the ball up and down the field without a problem. When they wanted to pass they passed and when they wanted to run they ran. The boys from the small school tried their hardest every play, you could see that, but there wasn't anything they could do. They were just outmatched.

Another beer? the bartender asked.

Another *cerveza*, Wallace said. When it was set down in front of him, he picked it up and slugged it back. It was cold and good and it almost made him forget about the mess of hell he was about to catch when he told Cindy the news. She didn't like him leaving, even if it was just for a day or two, even if it

7

was business, and she liked to lay it on thick.

You're gonna leave me here to fend for myself, she'd say. Leave me here with two kids to figure out by myself how the hell to make it all work.

I'm sorry, he'd say. It's not like I want to.

And that wouldn't be good enough. She'd learned how to rack up the guilt from the best in the business. Her mother was an all-world pro at playing that card. Kept her old man miserable his whole life until he just died one day. Was out in the front yard, mowing the grass, probably listening to her yell at him from the door, when he just flopped over.

The food came as he was just finishing up his second beer and thinking the whole thing over. The waitress stacked four Styrofoam boxes on the bar next to him and took his money. He was thinking about just taking off that night, not even saying goodbye to Cindy or the kids. It was a thought that struck him as pretty good. He knew it wouldn't have been the worst idea. He could just take off into the night and start over. After all, he'd done it before. Out of all the things he was good at, that was probably the best. Boss would try and track him down, but he'd give up after awhile. Or maybe not. But at least he wouldn't have to go back to Indiana, back to that hornet's nest.

But he thought better. He pictured Cindy sitting there at home, those two kids crying and carrying on, her on the phone with her mother and cursing his name. He thought of everything he'd left behind the first time and felt worse than he'd felt in years. You're already carrying a load, he thought to himself. No need to pile on more.

It was already dark when he pulled into his driveway. The kids were watching a show on the living room TV and barely looked up as he came in the door. How we doing? he said to them and didn't receive an answer. He carried the boxes of food into the kitchen and found Cindy there straining some spaghetti noodles in the sink. She turned and saw the takeout boxes and shook her head.

That's just great, she said.

Sorry, he said. Thought I was doing something thoughtful.

The kids came running and asked what was in the boxes. When he told them, the older one, the boy, let out a cheer and the girl stuck out her bottom lip like Wallace had done something horrible to her.

I don't want it, the girl said.

Well, Cindy said, we've got spaghetti too.

I don't want that either, the girl said.

Cindy looked at Wallace as if to say, look what you've done, and he shrugged and put the boxes on the kitchen table. The boy wasted no time and opened them one by one until he found the hamburger and fries. He was halfway through the hamburger when Wallace went over to Cindy and put his arms around her.

Hey darling, he said.

Don't hey darling me, she said. You went and ruined supper.

Nah, he said. I like to think I just added options.

Think what you want, she said. All I know is there better be grilled chicken in one of those.

You got it, he said and leaned in for a kiss. She

kissed him lightly, to let him know that all wasn't forgiven. Got it for you special, he said.

I don't care how you got it, she said. I just know you didn't get it out of the kindness of your heart. Isn't that right?

How you figure? he said. Guy can't do something for his girl?

He can, she said. Guy can do all kinds of somethings for his girl, but this guy doesn't do that unless he's got something to tell her that ain't gonna make her very happy.

Wallace knew there wasn't anything to say to that, so he grabbed his half of the chicken and rice and beans and had a seat next to his son, who had already moved onto his fries. Wallace grabbed a fork out of the drawer by the sink and started digging in. He leaned back in his chair and opened the fridge and grabbed a beer. Cindy and the girl joined them at the table and ate their food. Nobody said much of anything as they ate, except the boy, who wanted to tell Wallace and Cindy about the show he and his sister were watching on the TV.

After dinner Wallace picked up the takeout boxes and tossed them in the trash along with his empty cans of beer. The kids took off for the TV again and Cindy took the spaghetti she'd made and the sauce that was on the stove and put them in plastic containers and set those in the fridge.

You're going out of town, she said. I can see it written all over your face.

Just going to be a couple of days, he said.

That's Hoosier-speak, she said. We've been

together eight years now, Wallace. I know what it means when you say a couple of days. That means ten days. That means two weeks.

Maybe, he said. You never know.

You never know, she repeated. Ain't that something? We got two kids and you say you never know.

That's about all I can offer, Wallace said. I'm sorry, darling. There's not much I can do about it.

I can't stand that fucking pig, she said.

Don't say that, Wallace said.

I mean it, she said. I cannot stand that fucking fat pig. He doesn't give two shits about anybody, about family, about anything. Tells you to go here, go there, without so much as a fucking thought.

He's not that bad, Wallace said. Don't we live okay?

We live okay, Cindy said, but not that okay. Not okay enough that you can just take off for a couple weeks, a month, or whatever.

It won't be a month.

How do you know? Do you know?

I know, he said.

What's he have you doing? she said.

Construction, he said. Have to sit and meet with a couple of people.

Construction, she said. I bet. I bet that's what he's got you doing.

Cross my heart, he said and walked over to where she was standing and put his arms around her again and went in for another kiss. This one was better than the one before and he pushed his luck and kissed her one more time. She loosened up then and he reached down between her legs and pressed his fingers against her through her jeans.

Easy now, she said. You aren't off the hook yet.

No? he said. Still on the hook?

Still on the hook, she said and closed her eyes. So far on the hook.

How about that? he said and led her out of the kitchen and through the living room where the kids were sitting. We got to talk over a couple of things, he said to them, you guys hold tight, okay? They said they would and Wallace led Cindy down the hallway and into their bedroom. He closed the door behind them and unbuttoned her jeans and slid them down her legs and over her ankles and feet and tossed them onto the floor. On the hook still? he said, making his way up her thighs.

Oh, brother, she said. You don't even know.

Chapter 3

You never met Carp, huh?

No sir, the younger man named Lucrow answered. New to this.

That's right, Simmons said. Sometimes I forget.

They were driving down a dirt road outside of Asheville and taking note of how many driveways they had passed. The one they were looking for wasn't marked by anything but a rusted gate and it was hard to make out in the black of night.

Thing about Carp, Simmons said, is that he's not like anybody you ever laid eyes on.

How do you figure? Lucrow said.

He just ain't. He's just somebody you look at and you know there's something different.

I'm not sure we should be talking about this, Lucrow said.

No?

No. Don't reckon Boss would want us talking about his best man like this.

You got a lot to learn, Simmons said. You sign up and work for a couple months and think you know everything.

Six months.

Six months. There you go. You sign up and work for six months and think you know goddamn everything.

Gravel kicked up and clicked against the side of

the car as they passed a gate overgrown by weeds.

How many driveways has that been? Simmons asked, trying to get his eyes used to the dark.

Five, Lucrow said. We been past five gates.

You sure 'bout that?

Dead positive. I've got one of those photographic memories.

No shit? Simmons said. You really got one of those?

Swear on it, Lucrow said. You show me something, a book or a picture or a newspaper or whatever and I'll remember it 'til the day I die.

How about that.

Lucrow said, It's nothing special. Just a thing.

They drove past three more drives until they came to a gate on the right side of the road. The drive itself stretched about a hundred yards and took the two of them past a maze of burnt-out and rusted cars. As the headlights swept over them, they glinted dully and disappeared back into the dark. Past them was a small green house without even a single light shining. An old wooden sign hung off the porch and it said Carpenter.

Couple of things, Simmons said. There's a process that has to be followed here.

Got it, Lucrow said.

First things first, take your piece off. Lucrow gave Simmons a sour look and Simmons responded, You can't wear that thing in there. You take a piece in there and Carp's gonna know it. And you don't want to get him excited.

What's this guy's deal?

I told you, Simmons said. This isn't someone you want to fuck with. There's a process for a reason. Now. Take off your piece.

The two of them emptied their holsters of their revolvers and stashed them in the glove box. There was a box sitting in there and Simmons pulled the box out and opened it. He took out a pair of rubber gloves and handed another pair to the young man.

Put these on, he said.

Okay, Lucrow said.

Now, Simmons said, we're going to get in there and it's going to be unsettling. That's the only word for it. You're gonna think you're ready for this, but you aren't, okay? And you're going to lose it a little bit, but make sure you don't show it. Got it? Cause the last thing you want to do is get in there and let him see you losing it.

What am I going to see in there?

Simmons said, I'm not going to get into that. All I can tell you is this. Carp's a different kind of fella. This job's the only thing he lives for. He breathes it. What I'm saying is, he ain't one for Christmas cards, okay? He doesn't make small talk or head down to the store to buy cookies.

I guess I don't understand, Lucrow said and put on the second glove.

No, Simmons said. I guess you wouldn't.

They got out of the car and walked slowly up to the front door. It wasn't locked so they let themselves in. The house itself was clean, not a thing out of place. The first room they came to was the kitchen and when Simmons flipped the light switch Lucrow could see the sink was clear of dishes and the counters looked as if they'd been wiped that very evening. There was even a calendar on the wall, a normal looking one with a beagle dog for the picture.

Simmons called out, Carp. Carp, we're here with a job.

There was a hallway after the kitchen, but there were no pictures on the wall. Nothing on the walls. Lucrow snuck a look into the bedrooms they passed along the way and saw, the best he could, that they were empty too.

Carp, Simmons called out again. Carp, it's Reggie. I'm here with a buddy of mine to talk to you about a job.

Finally they came to the living room. It was neat, much like the kitchen, with the exception of a tray next to the couch that held several empty bottles of generic health shakes and meal supplement drinks. Littered among those bottles were bottles of prescription medications and plastic cups of water. There was a TV in the room but it wasn't turned on. The man who would have watched it, who was sitting in a recliner directly opposed to it, had a stark white complexion, his face covered in an unruly beard that fell down off his chin and over his hospital gown covered chest. His hair was in a similar state, grown out of hand and snaking the sides of his sunken face. In his arms, his thin and sickly arms, were IVs that wound around his chair and rose up and into clear bags hanging from a metal stand.

Oh, shit, Lucrow said. He looked at Carp and could instantly smell sickness and piss and shit. He looked just like a corpse he had seen in a ditch when he was only eight years old. Lucrow turned to Simmons and said, Is he alive?

He's alive. Calm the fuck down. Carp, he said, we're here with a job.

Carp, who had seemed catatonic until then, opened his eyes and stared at the two. They were glazed over and rimmed red as if he'd been asleep for days on end. A job, he said.

Help me get these things out, Simmons said to the young man and motioned to the IVs. He reached down and popped the first one out of Carp's right arm and then Lucrow, with some hesitation, got the other one in the left. He looked at Carp's forearms, bruised from the IVs, and at the crazy mess of veins.

A job, Carp muttered.

A job, Simmons repeated. We've got the details out in the car.

The two men lifted Carp out of his seat and carried him into one of the bedrooms off the hallway. There was a bed and a solitary dresser. Simmons looked through the drawers and found some underwear and an undershirt and a pair of jeans and socks and laid them out on the bed. He and Lucrow dressed Carp and then helped him into the adjoining bathroom.

Lucrow got Simmons' attention and whispered, Is he okay? as Carp teetered on the edge of the toilet, his eyes rolling wildly in his head. Cause, I mean, he doesn't look okay.

Seriously, Simmons said, rifling through the medicine cabinet and getting out a pair of scissors, you need to shut your fucking mouth already. I told you to cool it.

I'm cool, Lucrow said.

The fuck you are.

Simmons used the scissors and cut great bunches of hair off Carp's face and then his head. When that was done he found a razor and some shaving cream and gave Carp the closest shave he could.

What's this job? Carp asked, sounding more lucid. Where?

Indiana, Simmons said. Seymour, Indiana.

That's a twelve-hour drive, Carp said. Am I going alone or do I have a shotgun?

Wallace is going, Simmons said. He'll be down in the morning.

Wallace, Carp said, reaching up and touching his freshly shaven face. He lifted himself off the toilet and steadied himself at the sink. He gazed into the mirror as if he didn't recognize the face staring back. Details are in the car? he said.

In the car, Simmons said.

Then let's head to the car, Carp said.

The three of them walked to the car and Carp opened his door and let himself into the backseat. Simmons and Lucrow sat in the front and Simmons asked Carp if there was anything else he needed and Carp told him they needed to make a stop at the Wal-Mart.

Why the Wal-Mart? Lucrow said.

Shut up, Simmons said.

Carp reached into the front seat with a shaking, skeleton-like hand and asked for the folder. Simmons handed it back and then started the car. Carp asked for the overhead light to be turned on and after it was, he sat in silence and read the folder. The only sound was the sound of the motor and the sound of Carp cracking his neck. It was like the popping of an automatic rifle.

Need a cooler and a hacksaw, Carp said when they pulled into the Wal-Mart parking lot.

What's that? Lucrow said.

Cooler and a hacksaw, Carp said.

You need us to get you a cooler and a hacksaw? Lucrow asked.

That's what he said, Simmons said through gritted teeth.

Wait a second, Lucrow said. What kind of a cooler? And a hacksaw?

A hacksaw, Carp said. And any kind of a cooler. Just make sure it's big enough to hold a bowling ball.

A bowling ball?

Go ahead and shut the fuck up, Simmons said. He said a cooler and a hacksaw.

The two of them left Carp in the car and went into the Wal-Mart. It was nearly midnight so there weren't many people in the aisles, save for some lonely-looking older shoppers and the bored cashiers behind the registers. Some country music played over the sound system.

You need to learn your place, Simmons said. Can't go running your mouth like that.

Lucrow pointed at the doors and said, That guy is a goddamn maniac. He's certifiable. What in the hell is this all about?

He's the best guy we got, Simmons said, walking toward the back. Bar none.

Excuse me if I have a hard time believing that.

You're excused.

They came to the sporting goods section and found an aisle with nothing but coolers. There was every kind of cooler imaginable. Some had wheels and others had places where a drink could be rested. Finally they settled on a red Igloo cooler with a white top. A couple of aisles over was the tool section and they found a ten-inch Stanley hacksaw with a fixed frame. It was regularly seventeen dollars and fifty cents but was marked down to an even fifteen. A woman with a massive mole that spread from the corner of her eye to her left temple manned the checkout counter. That's a strange combination, she said, scanning the items.

You got that right, Lucrow agreed.

Whatcha got planned? the cashier said.

Don't know, Lucrow said. Bought 'em for the maniac we've got out in the car.

On the way back to the car, Simmons said, I know I said to cool it earlier. And I meant it. You need to lay off.

I hear you, Lucrow said.

No, Simmons. I don't think you do. You need to give the act a fucking rest.

Just as they had left him, Carp was in the back seat, staring straight ahead. Simmons opened the backdoor and showed him the cooler and the hacksaw. That work for you? he said. Carp said it did and Simmons stowed them away in the trunk of the car. All right, he said, getting behind the wheel again. Gonna stop over at Boss' and that'll be the end of the road for us.

Let me ask something, Lucrow said and turned around in his seat to face Carp, who looked at him without blinking.

Come on, Simmons pleaded. Don't do this, goddamn it.

No, Lucrow said. Don't worry about it, okay?

Just turn around.

Did you have a question? Carp said.

I had a question, Lucrow said.

He doesn't have a question, Simmons said. Forgive him, he's young and he's stupid.

No, Lucrow said, I got a question. I think we both have the same question, you and me. So tell me, he said, looking at Carp. What's up with the cooler and the hacksaw? Whatcha got planned with those things? Come on.

It's all right, Carp said.

It's not, Simmons said.

It really is, Carp said. It's all right. I'll tell you if you want to know.

I want to know, Lucrow said.

Stop it.

I really want to know.

Okay, Carp said. I'll tell you then.

I'm sorry, Simmons said. I'm sorry, Carp, this kid's new. Doesn't know his place.

I'm going to Indiana and finding a man named Yorkie Goodman, Carp said.

You two going hunting or something? Lucrow

asked.

I'm going to find him, Carp said, and I'm going to cut off his head. And I'm going to drive it right back here to North Carolina and hand it over to Boss. I'm going to give it to him as a gift. And I want it to be perfect.

Chapter 4

In the morning Wallace rolled out of bed and crept into the bathroom. He hadn't been able to sleep all night, so the world was blurry. To make sure Cindy didn't wake up, he closed the door behind him before turning on the shower.

It was a routine he had had to get used to. His first wife, Amanda, was the heaviest sleeper he'd ever known. He could've marched a band through the bedroom and the worst she would've done was roll over. But Cindy was considerably more difficult. She slept in fits, like a cat he would joke, and something as small as the squeak of a hinge would wake her right up.

When he was finished showering, he got dressed and quietly picked up the bag of clothes he'd packed the night before. He thought of at least leaning over Cindy and kissing her goodbye, but he wanted his exit to be as simple as possible so he let her sleep and went into the kitchen.

From the refrigerator he pulled a carton of eggs and two beers and from the cabinet a tall glass. It was a tradition he'd learned from his dad, a mechanic who got Wallace up early in the morning to help with repairs. It had been nearly unbearable working a shift before school, but it was made worth it when he had a chance at one of his dad's beers. Now Wallace poured the first beer into the glass and then cracked one of the eggs in after it. He swallowed it down and then did another the same way.

Liquid breakfast, his dad had called it.

The drive over to Boss' office took fifteen minutes, long enough for the quick buzz of the beer to take hold. As he pulled into the lot he was wondering what on earth Yorkie Goodman could have possibly done to get this kind of attention. It must've been something awful to necessitate getting Carp involved.

Boss' office was located in a room above a gym called Popeye's. When Wallace parked his truck and walked inside, he was greeted with the usual stink of stale sweat and smoke. Some days it was so bad it made his eyes water. It was early though and there were only a few boxers milling about, a Spanish kid on the speed bag and Popeye leading a trio through their warm-ups. He lifted his good eye, the one not covered by a patch, just in time to see Wallace and give him a nod as he climbed the stairs.

A receptionist named Candy sat outside Boss' office. She spent most of her time playing with her cell phone. She was kind enough, and sweet on Wallace, so he liked her all the same. When he came up that morning, she finished typing something on her keypad and gave him a movie-screen worthy smile. She was pretty in a traditional way, though her features were all on this side of severe.

Mornin' honey, she said to Wallace. How you holdin' up?

Fine as a peach, he said. Boss in?

He certainly is, she said. And expecting you.

Wallace walked past her desk to the door leading

into Boss' office. From outside he could hear Boss yelling into his phone. He turned the knob and let himself in.

Listen here, motherfucker, Boss said, we had us a goddamn deal. Where I'm from, that means you follow through. He saw Wallace and gestured for him to sit down in one of the chairs in front of the desk. As he did, his face grew darker shades of red. I don't give a shit, he spit, you told Lorna, no later than last week, that that fucking set was going to be in yesterday. Yesterday, he said, screaming and banging his fist on his desk, do you understand what the fuck yesterday means?

He slammed the phone down onto its base and beat the desk with his fist. Sweat had collected on his forehead and when he reached to wipe it away it was replaced immediately. Wallace had seen Boss worked up like this before and knew that when he was especially pissed off, he was capable of sweating for hours on end.

That sounded pleasant, Wallace said.

Wallace, Boss said, shaking his head, I got to tell you, there ain't a motherfucker left worth a shit. I mean that. The whole human race has gone to hell.

You're not going to get any argument there.

This jackoff, he said, pointing at his phone, doesn't know he just pissed off the wrong sonuvabitch. I can't handle it, Wallace. I can't stand it anymore.

What's this all about?

My wife, bless her dumb little heart, has gone furniture crazy.

Wallace tried his best to look surprised, but Boss' wife Lorna's spending sprees were hardly a secret in the organization. Lorna, twenty years Boss' junior, was blessed with an unrivaled ability to burn through money. When Boss met her, she'd been Topsy McGuire's girlfriend and she'd done everything in her power to waste every last cent he had to his name. After Boss had Topsy put down, he took a liking to her and moved her in. Not long after, she'd talked him into a koi pond stocked with hundreds of the most expensive fish. That kept her attention for the better part of a month before she got into tapestries. Her newest obsession was antique and high-end furniture, which had been rolling in day after day. Wallace and the other men had been all over the Carolinas, picking up custom pieces of furniture made of the heaviest wood.

This guy, Boss said, he's jerking me around. He was supposed to have a bedroom set, a four-poster, pair of dressers, old-fashioned mirror, nightstands, lamps, the whole nine yards, ready to be picked up yesterday.

Can't trust anybody, Wallace said.

Boss pointed at Wallace. You got that right, he said. You got that dead-to-rights, my friend.

The intercom on his desk interrupted him.

Carp is here, Candy said through the speaker.

Send him in, Boss said.

Hearing Carp's name made Wallace sick to his stomach. In all his years working for Boss he'd never gotten used to being around the man. He didn't seem human, never said more than a few words, and you could never tell what kind of thoughts were rolling around his head. Wallace had done close to a dozen jobs with him and still couldn't figure him out.

Carp walked through the door and Wallace realized, with cold certainty, that the expression on his face was the same as the one he'd worn, a few months before, when they'd held a local thug down and deposited a clip full of shells directly into his temple.

Boss, Carp said. Wallace.

Carp, Boss said, good to see you, buddy. Have you a seat.

He sat down in the chair next to Wallace's and crossed his legs. Wallace watched him and thought about how he looked like a machine.

All right boys, Boss said, you've both had a chance to look over your folders. It's a pretty straightforward job. Drive out to Seymour, do a little reconnaissance, take out the target, and bring back a trinket.

Sounds good, Wallace said.

Easy enough, Boss said. Carp, you have any questions?

No sir, Carp said.

Didn't figure you would, Boss said and then drummed his fingers on his desk. I don't think it's necessary for me to tell you this, but you two guys are the best I got. Just the fact that I got you two on this thing should tell you it's a big deal.

Wallace cleared his throat and said, I had a question about that, Boss. This fella, Yorkie, from his file he seems like a pretty regular guy.

I think that's a fair conclusion, Boss said.

27

There a reason we're on this? I mean, I'm fine with complications, but I like to know if there's a pile of shit before I step in it.

Carp turned his head without moving the rest of his body and glared at Wallace.

Listen, Boss said, when I say this is straightforward I mean *straightforward*.

I get that, Wallace said.

Like I said, you go and you do the job. Don't mess around with anything else. It shouldn't be that big of a deal and it shouldn't take that much work.

All right, Wallace said.

Okay, Boss said. Now, come and let me show you something.

The three of them walked out the side door of the office and followed a set of metal stairs into the hidden garage at the back of the building. It housed Boss' fleet of Jaguars – his babies, as he called them – and a few of the organization's customized wheels. Everything other than the sports cars were hulking SUVs outfitted with bulletproof glass and smuggling wells. Boss led Wallace and Carp past the usual suspects and to a newish, silver Ford.

I put a note in Carp's file, Boss said to Wallace. You got a stop to make along the way. There's a guy right outside of Indy who owes me a favor. In the trunk's four hundred pounds, he said, pulling a key fob from his pocket and clicking a button. The trunk opened and Wallace could see a small mountain of shrink-wrapped bricks of pot. You deliver and he'll pay and set you up with some tools.

Wallace sucked on his cheek and said, Good to

know.

Don't drive like idiots and you should be fine. Somebody asks questions, just tell 'em you two are brothers, Boss said and laughed.

Wallace looked at Carp's unchanging face and thought he looked more like a ghost in the dim light of the garage.

Well, Wallace said to him, am I driving or you?

I would prefer, Carp said in his usual, irregular cadence, if you took the first leg.

You got it, brother, Wallace said, taking the keys.

Chapter 5

Chief Dean set down the Styrofoam box from Hilliard's Bar & Grill and tossed his plastic fork into the trash. He'd barely made it through half of the soggy enchiladas he'd ordered in for dinner but was already possessed of a powerful case of heartburn.

Bockwinkel, he said and got the attention of his youngest deputy, give me one good reason we still order this bullshit food.

The deputy stopped shoveling tasteless rice into his mouth and shook his head. I couldn't even begin to tell you. With a shrug he said, Because it's there?

Because it's there, Dean said to himself.

The office was small enough that the different smells of their dinners were already beginning to mingle and sour the air. It was a forty-by-forty space with a pair of ten by ten cells in the back. Seymour was a quiet town and the jail was primarily used as a drunk tank or holding area until men sobered up or a dispute got settled. Dean threw his box away and walked over to the cells. He did so with a great limp in his right leg and it took a good, long time for him to reach the bars. Leaning against them, he stared out the window that looked over Main Street.

Finishing off the last scraps of his dinner, Bockwinkel said, Slow night.

Dean hustled himself and said, Every night's a slow night, Blaine. Sometimes I look at this place and wonder if it's just gonna stop breathing on us.

Town or the office?

Both. Neither. I don't know. Dean turned and watched Bockwinkel spill a forkful of food down the front of his uniform. A day hardly went by that he didn't wear a shirt with a stain on it. Dean's old drill sergeant had had a name for cadets like that – shitboxes. If he saw a speck of anything on their clothes, he'd get within inches of their faces and give them the spit shine treatment, screaming for them to get their shitbox asses in shape. The nickname had burrowed so deep in Dean's brain that he could barely look at Bockwinkel without thinking it to himself.

You wanna get a card game going? Bockwinkel said, scrubbing at his shirt with a napkin.

Shitbox.

Nah, Dean said. Least not yet.

As if he hadn't heard Dean's answer, Bockwinkel got a deck of cards out of his desk. He was a decent euchre player but dreadful at spades and poker. Dean and he usually played two hands apiece every night but Dean was getting tired of his deputy letting him win all the time. Such behavior was the mark of a kiss-ass and Dean didn't have any time for that.

Bockwinkel shuffled the cards and said, I got a good feeling about tonight. You ought to watch out, I'm likely to take a few paychecks.

Dean was about to tell Bockwinkel to go to hell when the dispatcher came through the radio on his belt. 808 reported at The Hideout, she said.

He clicked the send button on his unit. Jimmy Lee again?

You got it, she said.

Dean got his unit back on his belt and slowly walked over to get his squad car's keys from the hooks by the door. Bockwinkel was right at his heels. I'll take care of it, he said. No use you having to drag yourself over there to deal with Jimmy Lee.

Drag myself over there? Dean said.

I didn't mean nothing by it, Chief. Just meant it ain't worth the trip.

Dean knew it wasn't, but boredom had set in and he knew from a ways back that it could be a terminal condition if you didn't relieve it in time. The call was something of a monthly tradition: Jimmy Lee had been a championship kick-boxer back in the day and whenever his child support came due, and his old lady gave him a ring to put the screws to him, he'd go out, get sauced up, and start showing his moves off in whichever bar he happened to be settled into for the night.

Think I'll take my turn with Jimmy Lee, Dean said and went out the door.

Bockwinkel followed behind and that made Dean's day. He knew the deputies looked up to him and that sort of fondness filled him with pride. Anytime he decided to handle a situation himself the boys were more than eager to tag along and observe.

Driving over to The Hideout he knew full and well how things were going to play out. Jimmy Lee was a showoff and he was probably either at the bar or on the dance floor, kicking up a ruckus. There wasn't much danger as he was, by this time, liquored up to his gills. All Dean needed to do was apply a little force and the scene would be over in a hurry. Jimmy Lee, after all, was a washed-up fighter and didn't have much in the way of real and honest danger left in him.

We just going to bring him in? Bockwinkel asked as they were about a block away.

Something like that, Dean said. Reckon maybe we'll make an example.

They parked in front of the consignment shop on Vincennes and Dean sat and let the car idle. Across the street was The Hideout, a hole-in-the-wall neighbored on either side by antique shops the blue-hairs liked to visit during the day. The sign above the front door was half-lit in lights, the H and the d long-since extinguished, leaving a mess of vowels.

Dean could see right into the bar from where he sat. Maybe sixty yards away, near the bandstand, Jimmy Lee was stumbling around, a couple of his buddies holding him up and trying their best to drag him off.

Looks in rough shape, Bockwinkel said.

Dean agreed, but his mind was elsewhere. The position he was in left him with an ideal straight shot. Back in boot camp he'd been a hell of a sniper before his mom had written letters to get him a discharge. Most people round Seymour knew the former part of that and it was always whispered about that Dean had been something of a crack shot, the kind the Marines and Special Forces wrestled over. There were even tall tales about how he had been whisked off to hot spots around the globe to take out high value targets. Knowing full and well it was bullshit, Dean didn't mind letting people talk.

I reckon, Bockwinkel said in a whisper, you wouldn't have much of a problem picking him off from here. Is that right, Chief?

That's right, Dean said.

That'd be something to see.

A memory sparked in Dean from back in his glory days, before his knee was shot all to hell and he'd ended up the lawman of a town absent of crime. Looking at Jimmy Lee through the window, he remembered staring through his Leupold Mark 4 and lovingly adjusting the sight – like bringing a woman to the edge – and slowing his breathing down until there was nothing but him, the breeze, and the center of the target down-range.

Picking off Jimmy Lee would've been just about as easy as hitting one of those targets. Placing a round right in the center and hardly disturbing the paper at all.

Listen, Bockwinkel said, interrupting the memory, I'm just gonna run in and get this taken care of, Chief. Last thing you need to do is get into some kind of situation. With your knee and all.

Dean shot Bockwinkel a hard look. You wanna come in, he said, you come in. But stay the fuck out of my way.

When they walked into the bar, the music had already been shut off. There was just the sound of Jimmy Lee fighting off his friends, telling them he had the right mind to kick all their asses. Meeting Dean and Bockwinkel at the door was Patti Gage, the run-down owner and bartender.

Evenin', Chief, she said, exasperated, Jimmy Lee's

acting the idiot again.

Fair enough, Dean said, let's see what we can do.

Soon as Jimmy Lee saw Dean coming for him he shrugged off his friends and cracked his knuckles. He wasn't a big man – five-ten and a hundred and seventy pounds – but he was a born and bred fighter. In the Eighties he'd fought for nearly every kickboxing title in the area. Dean had witnessed him fight in the armory a few times and even seen him knock one of his opponent's nose crooked as could be. He knew he wasn't somebody to take lightly.

Jimmy Lee, Dean said, reckon maybe you've had a few too many.

Reckon it's none of your fuckin' business, he said and spit on the floor. Jimmy Lee reached down and grabbed his T-shirt at the bottom and pulled it up and over his head. His body hadn't aged particularly well, there were love handles and stretch marks running across his stomach, but you could tell that at one point he'd been a well-oiled machine.

Hate to be the one to tell you this, Dean said, but this here badge makes it my business.

Jimmy Lee didn't waste any more time. Drunkenly, but with enough poise to show he was experienced, he sprang forward and flicked a jab that barely breezed by Dean's face. Then another that hit clean and put him on his heels.

Chief, Bockwinkel yelled and reached for his gun.

Keep it holstered, Dean said, turning to him and holding up his hand, his nose already bleeding. I got this.

Jimmy Lee flicked another jab, his right leg

cocked and ready to unload, but Dean dodged and grabbed his wrist. When Jimmy Lee went to unlock it, Dean unpacked his nightstick in a fluid motion and swung it hard into Jimmy Lee's left knee. It hit and he buckled. Dean locked his arm under his chin and brought him down all the way. When they were both on the floor, Dean holding Jimmy Lee's neck as he writhed above him, Dean got a few hits in on his back and felt the body collapse into him.

Blaine, Dean said, get his arms around and in cuffs.

Bockwinkel did as he was ordered, making sure first that none of Jimmy Lee's friends were ready to make a move, and wrestled Jimmy Lee's arms behind his back. His skin was sweaty and cold and he got loose twice before Bockwinkel got the cuffs in place.

Dean let go and, with the help of a nearby stool, picked himself off the floor. Blood was streaming out of his nostrils and bottom lip, running down over his chin and neck and onto his uniform.

The voice that was always going in his head piped up and said, simply, shitbox.

Bockwinkel was getting Jimmy Lee to his feet. When he got there, Dean could see his face had gone blue and he knew he'd only been a few seconds away from crushing his windpipe or choking him out for good.

Patti came over and said, My God, Chief, thanks for coming.

You got it, Dean said and grabbed a napkin off the bar to wipe his face.

Can I get you anything? she said. Glass of water?

Ice? A beer or something?

Dean was about to say no thank you, but he paused. Jimmy Lee was laying across the bar and still fighting to get his breath back. You know, Dean said, most times I'd say no, but I could use one right about now.

Patti grabbed a bottle of Budweiser from behind the bar and popped the top. Dean took it with a nod and tipped it back. The beer was colder than any he'd ever tasted before and it slid down in a hurry. Tell you what, he said, putting it down, you better make that two.

Chapter 6

The music piping through Rocket's Diner was turned down so low that Wallace could barely hear more than a hum, but he could tell it was country, new country, the kind that didn't sound like anything at all.

I just don't understand, he said to Carp across the table, how we can drive twelve hours in a car and you don't even care to turn on the radio.

I've no use for it, Carp said and continued to tear his toast into bits. His plate held only a single egg and five slices of toast and was already covered in crumbs. Music is a distraction. I've no use for distraction.

Distraction? It's music. It just makes no sense to me, Wallace said, dragging his fork around. How can you sit in silence that long?

I could handle silence right now, Carp said.

Wallace dropped his fork on his plate. He was about to tell Carp that, on second thought, he wouldn't mind some silence himself, when the waitress returned with a pot of coffee. She was young, maybe seventeen, and Wallace had stopped himself from asking her why she wasn't in school.

Coffee? she said.

Yes ma'am, Wallace said and held out his cup.

What about you, honey? she said to Carp and got an emotionless stare in return. All right then, she said before walking off.

Doesn't like music, Wallace said and blew on his drink, doesn't want more than one cup of coffee. You, my friend, are a piece of work.

It disturbs the nerves.

What?

The nerves, Carp said. It affects the nerves.

Wallace stared at Carp. Under the fluorescent lights he looked like a spot on a wall that hadn't been painted yet. During their drive the day before, as Carp sat in the passenger seat and stared straight ahead, seemingly never blinking, it had occurred to Wallace that Carp was a member of a completely different species. Every time he tried to start up a conversation, Carp was quick to cut it off. When he reached for the knob of the radio, Carp shut it down just as fast. He knew it was in his best interest to leave him alone, but Wallace was tired and felt prickish.

You ask me, he said, I can't go a day without coffee. Need a cup every few hours. It's like gas for the engine.

It replicates the affects of adenosine.

Adenosine? What the fuck are you talking about?

Carp picked up his nearly empty mug and swirled what was left. Caffeine, he said. Its molecular structure works as a stand-in for the chemical adenosine. It builds and builds until the body is ready for rest. For sleep. Caffeine blocks it.

Wallace nodded and took a sip of his coffee, burning his tongue in the process. All right, he said.

More than eight ounces, Carp continued, and you're overstressing the system. Rest is natural. Rest is good. If you don't listen to your body when it wants to rest, then you're in danger of a malfunction.

The waitress appeared in Wallace's peripheral vision and he called for their check. He said, That's fascinating, Carp. Good to know you're focused.

The question, Carp said, as the waitress brought over the ticket, is whether you're focused, Wallace.

Excuse me?

Carp picked his folder off of his seat in the booth and set it on the table. He tapped it with his finger and said, I need to know that you're not going to be distracted.

I'm solid, Wallace said. No reason you even have to ask.

Opening the folder, Carp came to a page and read without emotion: Bill Wallace is originally from Hayden, Indiana, roughly eight miles east of Seymour. In 1999 he walked into the Seymour City Jail and shot prisoner Terry Wilcox at point-blank range. Wilcox, at the time, was suspected of sexually assaulting Christie Wallace, Bill's sister. In the process, Wallace substantially wounded then-deputy Stephen Dean via gunshot to the right knee.

What the fuck is that? Wallace said.

Carp went on: Shortly thereafter Wallace relocated to Raleigh, North Carolina with operations, leaving behind wife Carol Wallace, 46.

Wallace reached for the folder, but Carp swept up his knife and slammed it into the table between Wallace's middle and ring fingers.

Give me that, you sonuvabitch, Wallace said.

This is my folder, Carp said. It was given to me by Boss. You have your orders. I have mine.

Wallace kept his eyes focused on Carp's. They looked back at him, blank and uncaring. That's none of your business, he said.

It is my business, Carp said. It's also my business how you're going to behave on this job. If I am partnered with someone who's going to cause difficulties, I need to know.

Difficulties?

The waitress came close enough to see the knife and turn away.

I've been told, Carp said, that if you stray, if you try and contact your wife, that it's my first priority to cut you and her down.

Wallace pulled his hand back slowly. First priority? he said

First, Carp said.

Wallace threw some money down on the check and said, Lucky for you, I'm not planning anything. But, he said, for the record, you don't have balls big enough to finish that job.

Carp let go of the knife, leaving it to stand alone in the table. He blinked and then nodded. I assure you, he said, that wouldn't be a problem.

Without so much as another word Wallace and Carp left the diner and returned to the Ford in the parking lot. Wallace got behind the wheel and, before Carp could even strap in, he turned on the radio. Carp looked at it and then at Wallace, who was busy turning the volume up.

The house was twenty minutes away in the Indianapolis suburb of Broad Ripple. It sat at the end of the main strip, which was filled with bars, restaurants, and record shops. Saturday morning traffic was already picking up and young people were crowding the sidewalks. Wallace pulled up and fed a meter a pocketful of quarters and the pair walked down the strip to the beat-down house on the edge.

Its lot was beset with unmowed grass and weeds, the siding covered in half-finished pieces of graffiti. The mailbox by the road had been defaced so that the old label "The Smiths" now read "The Shits." Wallace pointed at it and got Carp's attention.

We've got some jokers here, he said.

Carp grunted and continued toward the house.

First Wallace tried the doorbell but it wasn't working. He knew there were people home from the sounds coming from inside. It was like a war in there, the echoes of gunshots and explosive rumbles from the TV.

He knocked hard and somebody looked out through the broken shade of a window. A few seconds later the door opened a crack and an eye peered out. Yeah? the owner of the eye said.

We're here to see Sweater, Wallace said.

Okay. And who're you?

Friends of a friend, Wallace said.

The door closed and he heard the chain on the door being unhooked. The noises ceased and whoever was at the door told somebody else to shut up before opening and gesturing for Wallace and Carp to come inside.

It was Sweater, Wallace knew that much from a picture provided in his folder. He had long, blonde dreadlocks tied back and a chinstrap beard grown out of control. He looked even younger than he had in his picture, which Wallace didn't think was possible.

How's it going? Sweater said, nodding in such a way that Wallace knew he was high off his ass.

Good, Wallace said and surveyed the room. There were two men, one fat, one thin, sprawled out on a sectional couch, game controllers in their laps. Paused on the TV was a first-person shooter game. The coffee table, the kind that Sweater's mom had no doubt handed down, was covered in buds, rolling papers, lighters, and cans of PBR.

So you work for Boss? Sweater said.

Carp bristled. Leave him out of it, he said.

Don't mind him, Wallace said, he's not the most personable guy. You're Sweater, I'm guessing.

You got it.

The two men on the couch unpaused their game and again the room was filled with the sounds of war. They hammered on their controllers and stopped only to drink their beers or pass a small, handcrafted piece back and forth.

Sweater plopped down next to them on the sectional and took his turn, sucking in a healthy hit. When he exhaled, a long, thin line of smoke slipped out of his mouth and lingered in the air. You guys need anything? he said as it dissipated. Beer? Hit?

Sure, Wallace said and looked at Carp. He didn't need to hear an answer to know Carp wasn't partaking. Wallace sat down on the edge of the couch and took the piece from Sweater, who jumped up and grabbed a pair of beers from the fridge. He gave the first to Wallace, who was taking his third hit, and offered the other to Carp. Carp took it, studied the label, and set it down.

Wallace finished with the piece and handed it back to Sweater who said, No offense, but I didn't know what to expect out of you guys. You hear there's a shipment coming in this big and you don't have any idea who the motherfuckers gonna be bringing it. He lit the piece and inhaled. Usually it's a bunch of toughs.

You don't think we're a couple of toughs? Wallace said.

Sweater coughed and laughed. He looked at Wallace. You seem cool, man, he said and then turned to look at Carp. Your boy here's quiet though.

He's a motherfucking zombie, one of the men playing the game said, sending Sweater and his other friend into laughter.

No offense, Sweater said when he was done. I mean, you just got that look about ya, man.

Carp looked at Wallace and said, We have places to be.

Wallace nodded and reached for the piece again. You're right, he said. My partner here has a point. Sweater, he said, we need to get this show on the road.

Hold on, Sweater said. Hold on just a second here. He snatched the piece back and set it on the table. I get that, man. I get that you don't have time to sit here and fuck around, but there's something I want to talk to you about. Something I want you to take back to Boss.

All right, Wallace said. We're listening.

Okay, Sweater said. Between y'all and me, I'm

getting tired of working with my distributor. Motherfucker takes forever between product deliveries. Gives me shit left and right. Got so bad that we've had to start hiding our supply. Had to pad our inventory, so to speak.

The thin man playing the video game reached over and bumped fists with Sweater. Wallace saw a tattoo on his forearm that read KILL OR DIE.

So, Sweater said, when you get back, let Boss know I'm interested in working some things out. Cutting out the middleman, if you know what I mean.

I know what you mean, Carp said.

We know what you mean, Wallace said. That's all good and dandy.

We got big plans, Sweater said and reached for a bud and a rolling paper. He deftly separated the seeds and filled the paper with green. When he was finished, he rolled the paper and licked it to seal the joint. I know you're probably looking around and thinking we're small-timers, and that's fine, but we got bigger things coming. Ain't that right?

Sweater's friends barked like dogs in unison.

Sound good? Sweater said.

Sounds perfect, Wallace said. Just perfect. Now, let's get some shit out of our trunk.

Sweater and his friends got into Sweater's SUV a few minutes later and pulled out of the driveway and waited for Wallace and Carp to follow. Sweater's driving was erratic and the red SUV swerved in and out of lanes as they got on the loop around Indy. They circled the city until they were on the Southside and took an exit into Greenwood. It was a nice neighborhood, one that Wallace had spent some nights in a lifetime before, filled mostly with family homes and franchise restaurants. Wallace watched it all go by and couldn't help but sink into a feeling of déjà vu. Coming back to Indiana after all this time had woken something in him, though he couldn't tell yet what that something was.

Their destination was a storage facility called Self-Storage and, after Sweater had swiped a fob to open the outer gate, they followed him until they came to Unit 28. Sweater and his friends got out and unlocked the padlock on the metal pull-down gate. Wallace and Carp joined them inside and saw that most of the contents was covered in plastic tarps.

Close that door, Sweater said and gestured to Wallace. After he'd done it, one of the men turned on a flashlight and the dark retreated. The other pulled off a tarp. Under it was a small mountain of pot and an even smaller pile of cash. In the corner, beneath another tarp, was a cache of weapons and ammunition. I was told you brought four hundred and that you need some cash and the rest in guns.

That was the deal, Carp said.

What you need? Sweater said, walking over to the weapons. We got some semis, some sawed-off motherfuckers.

Just a couple of pieces, Wallace said. Nothing major.

Carp looked at Wallace, his expression unchanging. Wallace knew though that he'd stepped out of line somehow.

I'll take a piece, Carp said, and a pump-action.

870 if you've got it.

870? Sweater said and looked at his friends, who shrugged. Maybe, he said, you ought to come have a look.

Stepping past the bricks of pot, Carp joined Sweater by the stockpile and quickly picked up a Remington pump-action. He showed it to Sweater and then his friends. 870, he said.

Well, Sweater said, fuck me. I don't know shit about guns 'cept for how to point and shoot 'em.

Wallace joined Carp by the cache. He knew without a doubt it was in his best interest to get more than a piece now. Carp's selection of the Remington told him he'd better plan for a little bit more than what his folder had laid out. He grabbed a Desert Eagle and a few boxes of ammunition. Then a Bushmaster.

That's a lot of gun, Carp said.

Motherfuckers beware, Sweater said.

Better safe than sorry, Wallace said to an unblinking Carp, that's my motto.

Tell them to unload the product, Carp said to Wallace.

You heard him, Wallace said to Sweater and his friends. If you could clean out the trunk we'd be most appreciative.

Sweater and his friends went to work. With the gate to the unit opened, Sweater backed the Ford up to the entrance. Five minutes later the bricks had been added to the small mountain in the middle of the unit and Wallace and Carp had loaded their weapons and pocketed their payment.

Let's talk specifics, Carp said to Sweater. Close the door.

Sweater motioned to one of his friends and he pulled the metal gate shut. It was dark again except for the flashlight. The pile of pot separated them from Wallace and Carp.

Tell you what, Sweater said, I like your guys' style. You ever think about going independent?

We're listening, Wallace said.

Way I see it, we're all making pawn money right now. I mean, we live good, but we could live better. You know what I mean?

I know what you mean, Carp said.

Good. Then how about we say adios to the big motherfuckers and carve this area up for ourselves? We got the brains and you two mean motherfucking business. What do you say?

Wallace looked at Carp, who was barely lit in the dark. He was holding the pump-action at his side. Well, he said to Carp, what do you say?

Carp gave the signal and Wallace fired a half dozen rounds into Sweater's friends.

They slammed into the metal gate and slumped down onto the concrete.

Somewhere around the third or fourth shot Sweater gathered himself together enough to reach into his baggy jeans for his piece. Carp took his time walking toward him. The flashlight in Sweater's hand was racing erratically around the unit and Wallace could barely see as Sweater pulled a snub-nose out and cocked the hammer. Carp had reached him by then and knocked the flashlight out of his hand with a simple swipe.

The light died.

Now, now, Wallace heard Carp say in the dark.

The gate trembled like Sweater had been pushed up against it. His gun fell to the floor and skittered away.

Open your mouth, he heard Carp say. Go ahead, take it.

Sweater choked and screamed and begged wordlessly as Carp asked him, Now, who's a big man?

Carp pulled the trigger before Sweater could even answer.

Chapter 7

Boss was in the corner of the sparring ring, wrenching his head and working the kinks out of his long arms. All other activity in the gym had paused when Boss climbed between the ropes. All the young fighters and trainees knew he was a hard-ass from way back and wanted to watch. Popeye never got tired of telling them, as he held the heavy bag, that Boss could've been an all-time great.

Simmons and Lucrow were standing at ringside, the former nursing a cup of coffee and the latter sucking down a pouch of candy. I don't see it, Lucrow said between swallows. Boss looks tough, but he don't look like a champ.

Simmons looked into the ring and saw that Boss had heard his partner. Popeye was slicking him down, and Boss looked focused, but he glanced over at Simmons and gave him the briefest of smiles.

Maybe, Simmons said, but you need to shut the fuck up for once. Maybe focus more on candy and less on moving your trap.

Sure, Lucrow said, his mouth half-full. I'm just saying though.

At Boss' side, in the corner, was his nineteen-year-old stepson Abel. He was small, slight, and carried an unhealthy complexion. Most of the time he holed himself up in his room and was content to play on his computer, but his mom had begged Boss to

51

take an interest and man him up.

Abel, Boss said, throwing some shadow-punches, Abel, my boy.

Yeah? he said weakly.

I want you to take note. Watch how I keep my guard up. Always up, Abel. You lower that sonuvabitch, you're gonna be picking yourself up off the floor.

Guard up. Sure.

And lead with your left. With the jab. Gives your dominant arm room to work.

Lucrow almost choked on his candy and said, This kid's gonna be fighting Mike Tyson before the day's out.

Simmons gave him a shot in the side with his elbow.

Boss looked at the pair, then to Popeye. Your boy ready? he said.

Popeye gestured to the sparrer across the ring. His name was Domingo and he was one of the gym's up and comers. Sported quick feet and even quicker hands. In the locker room he'd started referring to himself as The Flurry and telling everyone who'd listen he was destined for the big show. He knew the fastest way to get there was to spar Boss and give him a good go of it. That meant Boss' attention and his sponsorship, so when Popeye asked him to get in the ring, he was more than ready.

Ding ding, Popeye said.

Boss lumbered deliberately out of the corner while Domingo raced over and met him a few steps in, wasting no time peppering Boss with jabs. Three, four, upwards of a dozen, none of them landing with any kind of force or meaning. Boss knew what he was doing. He'd seen it before. Padding his punch totals. Glancing shots off the shoulders and elbows, swats that amounted to next to nothing.

You worry about stats, Boss said to himself. Keep on thinking numbers.

Domingo shot another needle of a jab that Boss caught with his guard and Boss carefully positioned himself. Already he'd cut the ring off, leaving Domingo to blade his feet with the neutral corner at his back.

Tell me, Boss heard Lucrow say outside the ring, does Boss actually throw any punches or does he just walk around?

Sure, Boss said. I'll throw a couple.

The first jab was slow, but it rocked Domingo back on his left and then Boss motioned like he was gonna unleash the right and Domingo was almost in the ropes. One punch and the kid had already ceded five feet of ground.

A second later and Boss could tell that Domingo had realized his mistake, but Boss slid in as he tried to escape by wheeling his three hundred pounds into his path, like a tractor trailer cutting off a compact. Two steps and Domingo was cornered, all the flurry of his steps and jabs completely useless.

Here you go, Boss said, flicking a paw out just enough so that Domingo dropped his guard and moved his head right in line for a quick cross.

The cross hit and Domingo made a sound like a deep cough.

And now, Boss thought, the body.

Out of desperation Domingo's guard went up and Boss wormed a left into his ribs. Domingo recoiled, overreacted, and a right hit sharp into his kidney.

Boss sped up.

A left.

A right.

Domingo convulsed in one direction and then the other.

The movement had always reminded Boss of a juggler who'd come to his school when he was just a boy and performed with a bunch of colorful scarves that leapt into the air and fell delicately back to his hands, the pair of them working in perfect unison.

A left, Boss thought, the scarves firmly in mind, a right. A left, a right, rhythm, rhythm, rhythm.

So focused was Boss that he didn't see the trickle of blood work itself out of Domingo's mouth, or notice him go limp against the ropes. The only thing that broke his concentration was Popeye flying in and squeezing his way between them and prying Boss out of the corner.

I said, Popeye shouted, that's fucking enough.

Boss moved to the center of the ring and watched Domingo crumple to the mat as Popeye tried to lift him. Domingo was dazed and his face had the washed-out look of a man who was going to be pissing blood the better part of a month.

Abel, Boss said, catching his breath, you take note?

The boy shrugged and then gave him a half-hearted thumbs-up.

Goddamn it, Boss said. What the hell am I gonna do with you if you won't even try and give a shit?

How about adoption? the young man said.

Boss turned to ringside. Lucrow smiled as he finished off his candy. Simmons was busy acting like he didn't know him at all.

For a second Boss stood there rubbing his sweat-covered stomach with his glove. Then he said, Abel, step in here, son. And you, he said, pointing at Lucrow, join us for a minute.

Me? Lucrow said.

Yeah, Boss said. Help me out real quick.

Lucrow did as he was asked and climbed onto the apron and into the ring. Boss held out his gloves and Lucrow, relieved, helped him take them off. Underneath Boss' taped hands were bright red and he exhaled happily as he flexed them. When he was done he clapped Lucrow's shoulder and said, I need your help.

You name it, Lucrow said.

All right, Boss said, Abel, I want you to learn something here. Your mother told me, come hell or high water, I was supposed to make a man out of you.

You got your work cut out for you, Lucrow joked.

Boss grinned at him and then turned to Abel. You see what happens when you're weak? This man, this employee of mine has no respect for you.

Well, Lucrow said, I wouldn't say that.

Sure, Boss said. Be honest. It's good for the boy to hear. Tell him.

Lucrow looked at Abel, who seemed about as bored and passionless as anybody he'd ever laid eyes on. You sure? Lucrow asked.

Completely, Boss said. Tell him how it is.

All right, he said. Abel, he said, I don't respect you.

Come on now, Boss said, wrapping his beefy arm around Lucrow's shoulder. Lucrow could feel the heat pulsing off him and could smell his sweat. Tell him like you mean it.

All right, Lucrow said and pointed at the boy. I don't have a fucking shred of respect for you.

Still, Abel didn't say anything. He didn't even seem to register what Lucrow had said.

Abel, Boss said, say something.

What? Abel said.

Anything, Boss said. Tell him to go fuck himself. Lucrow laughed at that and Boss responded with a grin. Go on, he said to Abel. Tell him.

Go fuck yourself, Abel said halfheartedly.

That's better, Boss said. Now, with more meaning.

Go fuck yourself, Abel said, his voice rising slightly.

Now, Boss said, punch him in the fucking gut.

Lucrow shrugged off Boss' arm but Boss was quick to drape it over him again. I'm not gonna fight your fucking kid, he said.

I'm not asking you to fight him, Boss said.

Abel watched them, his hands still dangling at his sides.

Well? Boss said.

I'm not gonna punch him, Abel said.

Why not?

Because. He's bigger than me. He's older.

Abel.

I'm not going to, Abel said. I'm not gonna fucking punch him.

Boss felt Lucrow about to fight off his arm again and in one motion grabbed his collar and drove his right hand into his stomach. Boss did it like he'd been taught – to punch through his target – and he drove it until he could feel the soft and squirming parts of Lucrow moving around his knuckles.

Lucrow collapsed onto the mat. Not long after, he vomited up all of the candy he'd been eating and kept on vomiting until he started to dry-heave. Boss pointed at him on the ground and yelled at Abel, Get over there and kick this motherfucker.

Fuck you, Abel said.

Fuck me? Boss said. Fuck you. Fuck you, you sniveling little goddamn coward. Boss kicked Lucrow in the ribs and looked back to his stepson. That motherfucker said he didn't respect you and you're gonna stand there and take it?

At first Abel started to back away but then, like he was being pulled by some kind of force, he drew closer. He looked at his stepfather and then at Lucrow on the mat. Boss nodded and Abel drove the tip of his tennis shoe into Lucrow's back.

Lay the fuck off, Lucrow screamed, his voice choked. Come on.

Boss stomped him a couple of times, as if by example, and then moved out of the way to let Abel take his turn. Simmons was up on the apron and considering stepping in, but Boss shot him a look and he climbed back down. Abel started to stomp Lucrow, slowly at first, then quickening in tempo.

Goddamn, Abel said like a mantra, motherfucker, goddamn, motherfucker.

When he was finished, Lucrow was sprawled out, one hand resting on a rope, his face bloodied and dripping onto the canvas. Boss stared down at him and then pulled Abel in for a hug. Good boy, he said.

They were interrupted when Boss' receptionist peeked her head out the door to his office and yelled down to him that he was wanted on the phone.

Who the fuck is it? he asked.

Wallace, she answered.

All right, Boss said. Abel, come with me. Popeye, get this shit cleaned up.

Popeye was still in the other corner, tending to Domingo. He had his hand on the fighter's chest and could feel the shallowness of his breathing. All right, Popeye said. Sure thing.

Boss and Abel exited the ring and climbed the metal stairs leading up to Boss' office, their steps tracking prints of the young man's blood the whole way. When they got into Boss' office, he fell into his chair and pulled a towel from one of his drawers. He looped it about his neck and mopped sweat off his face and arms.

You know what? he said as he reached for the phone.

What? Abel asked.

I'm proud of you. Damned, damned, damned proud of you.

Abel grinned.

Yeah? Boss said into the phone.

It's Wallace, said the voice on the other line. Thought we'd let you know the business in Indy is done.

Fantastic. No complications, I presume?

None at all. Flipped on the GPS so you can let the people know where to look for the storage unit.

Is it contained? Boss said. Or do you think they were squirreling somewhere else too?

No, Wallace said. Pretty sure it was just this one. Money's there. Everything else too.

Good, Boss said, looking across the desk at Abel. The boy had his legs crossed and was studying the sole of his sneaker, running his fingernail through the lines of it and cleaning out the blood. So, Boss said, onto the next one.

That's right, Wallace said and paused. After a deep breath he said, I got to ask you something.

All right. Shoot.

Carp's folder had some info on me.

Sure.

Sure? Boss heard Wallace's cheek bristle against the phone. Cause it kind of pissed me off.

Well, then get unpissed. There were variables in this job. You knew that. No reason Carp shouldn't know it too.

I guess I can see that.

Good thing your job's not to fucking guess, Boss said. Good thing your job is to get the job done, huh?

Guess so, Wallace said.

Anything else?

Nope, Wallace said. I'll call in a couple of days.

Boss said, Good, and hung up the phone.

Everything cool? Abel said, starting to pick at the sole of the other sneaker.

Everything's cool, Boss said. Everything's real fucking cool. Now, he said, let's have a talk. You and me.

Okay. What about?

About respect, Abel. About how you can't let anybody look down on you. If there's one thing I ever teach you, it's that.

Okay.

Like that motherfucker, Boss said and pointed in the direction of the gym, that jackoff had no right to talk shit to no one. You included.

Got it.

You need to get it. You need to get that real straight. If I pulled half the pussy-ass shit you do, my dad would've beat me right to death. Wouldn't of thought twice about it. One day, back when I was twelve years old, I came home after losing a fight. You want to know what my dad said?

Abel finished with his sneaker and held up a finger. Under the nail was a thick line of blood. What'd he say?

He didn't say anything, Boss said. He took my ass out into the yard and beat the living hell out of me. Said afterwards if I ever came home the loser of a fight I might as well not come home at all.

That's pretty extreme, Abel said.

Boss pulled at the tape on his right hand and then on his left. He jerked a knot in my tail. That's why I am where I am, Abel. It's cause of that lesson, cause I learned to respect myself.

All right.

Don't say all right if you don't mean all right, Boss said, dropping the tendrils of tape into a pile on his desk. If there's anything I know, it's that you can't take back the shit you've said and done.

Chapter 8

After they'd taken their cut and reloaded their weapons, Wallace and Carp got back in the Ford, only this time Wallace gave Carp the keys and settled into the passenger seat. He was still somewhat high and more than a little regretful. He'd liked Sweater all right in the short time he'd known him.

Pull over here, he told Carp a few blocks from the onramp to the interstate.

We're close to the scene of the crime, Carp said.

Wallace said, I need some beer.

Gas stations have security cameras.

True, Wallace said, and the fact remains I still need some beer.

Carp wordlessly pulled the car into a Sunoco station and Wallace hopped out and strolled into the convenience store. It was early afternoon and people were there on their lunch breaks. He pushed through them to a section near the back called The Beer Cave and picked out a twelve-pack of Coors.

When he returned to the car, Carp said, You're not drinking those in the car.

Says who? Wallace said, tearing open the case. Before Carp had gotten back on the road he'd wrestled the first can out and popped its top. He drained half of it in one gulp and pointed at the exit. Here we go, he said.

The route was one Wallace knew better than

most. Back when Boss had worked out of Southern Indiana, before the business got too big and too heavy, Wallace had run I-65 South three to four times a week. Most of the time it was dope, fifty to a hundred pounds a shot, and the run to Seymour – right at sixty miles from Indy – took Wallace something like thirty to forty minutes if conditions were right. Louisville – a little over a hundred miles – got to be, in his heyday, an hour and ten minute sprint.

But Wallace knew he was in for a crawl with Carp driving. In all the jobs they'd done, he'd never seen Carp break a single traffic law or even nudge above the speed limit. Seymour was going to take an hour, if not longer, and he intended to kick back and enjoy himself.

By the time they got on I-65 he had his second beer opened and resting between his legs. It was cold and already he was feeling better. Coors reminded him of his stepdad and how he'd wake Wallace up on the weekend with a bowl of cereal and a pop-top. From the age of eight on he'd spent almost every Saturday on his stepdad's two-seater out on the pond, the two of them with their lines in the water and the cooler at their feet.

Nostalgia washed over Wallace as he watched the scenery. There was nowhere in the world he was more familiar with than this countryside. It was as if the towns and people had been put on pause after he'd left. The colorless sky was typical of an early fall Hoosier day, with large fists of clouds that gathered and dissipated without so much as a warning or reason. Even some of the billboards remained from his past.

Stop At Boot City.

A Child Isn't A Choice.

He tipped back his beer and wondered what else hadn't changed.

About an hour later they pulled into the outskirts of Seymour and stopped at a rundown motel called The Sunrise Inn. Wallace had driven by it at least a thousand times and never considered that someday he'd stay there. He waited in the car and finished off his ninth beer while Carp paid for a room.

The room was small with a pair of twin beds, an old TV set with tarnished knobs, and on the wall a cheap tapestry of an Indian chief astride a valiant-looking white horse. Wallace recognized it as the kind Hoosiers bought at fairs or festivals for ten bucks a pop.

Look how proud he is, Wallace said and pointed at the tapestry. Look how brave.

Carp didn't look. He was busy examining the pump-action he'd taken from the storage space, cleaning from its barrel Sweater's blood and spit. You're drunk, he said.

Wallace reached into his case and pulled out his next to last beer. True story, he said.

You're endangering the job, Carp said.

We don't have a job tonight, he said and opened the can. Tomorrow we work reconnaissance.

And you'll be hungover.

Wallace sank down on his bed. No, I'll be ready to go. Ready to check out this Yorkie Goodman character.

Carp didn't respond. He pulled back the pump-action and its click filled the room.

Yorkie, Wallace said again, pleased with the sound of it. Yorkie.

When he woke a few hours later his mouth was dry and tasted awful. Carp was lying on top of his bed, his hands folded on his chest and his eyes wide open. Wallace got up and stumbled into the bathroom to turn on the faucet. He stuck his mouth under the water and drank until he felt sick.

What're you up to? he said to Carp as he dried his face with a hand towel.

Visualizing, came the answer.

Visualizing? Wallace sat down on the edge of his bed and bent down to pull on his boots. What're you visualizing?

Carp took a deep breath and blinked his eyes. We're outside of Yorkie Goodman's house. We're watching him talk on the phone. He's pausing to take a drink.

That sounded good to Wallace so he retrieved his last beer. It was warm but he choked it down regardless. That's wonderful, he said. I'm gonna scare up some dinner. You want in on that?

No, Carp said. I'd like to finish.

Suit yourself, Wallace said and walked to the door. Outside the sky was dark except for a sliver of red to the west. This side of town was the neglected part, so most of the streetlights were dead and shadows covered everything except for a restaurant a mile down the road. Wallace could make it out – a Dairy Queen he'd eaten at long ago. Tossing his spent beer can into the parking lot he began his hike on the gravel shoulder.

Few cars passed. A truck honked at what Wallace could only assume was him. He'd been there before, behind the wheel and looking out at some poor asshole hoofing it down the line. He stopped walking. The world kept moving and he drunkenly staggered. He smelled himself, under his arms, his hands. The smell was a mixture of sour, of sweat and booze, and smoke.

His phone buzzed in his pocket. He half-expected it to be Boss when he dug it out of his pocket, but it was his wife. The picture on the screen was of her and the kids on the sand at Myrtle Beach, a vacation they'd taken that summer.

Yello, he said.

Hello? she said, confused. Honey?

You got it, he said. What's shaking?

I don't like the sound of your voice, she said. He could hear the kids running around in the background. You're drunk, she said. Are you drunk?

I'm a little drunk, he said, starting to walk again. I'm not gonna lie to you.

Goddamn. I thought you were there to work, not get fucked up.

Cindy, he said. I just got here. Lay off. I'm fine.

She huffed over the line and one of the kids, the boy, ran into the room and yelled out that he'd stubbed his toe. He'd always been dramatic, quick to tears. You okay? she said and the boy told her he was not. I swear, she said, sometimes this place is too much.

I hear you, he said.

Don't tell me that, she said. Don't take off cross the country and pretend like you've got a house to take care of.

That's not what I'm saying, he said and pulled the phone away from his ear. He looked at it like he wasn't sure what it was and brought it back. I mean, I'm sorry.

All right, she said. Thank you. How's Indiana?

He looked ahead at the Dairy Queen and watched a car pull through the drive-thru. He took a long sniff of the air and smelled dust and the far-off hint of charcoal. Like I never left, he said.

Well, she said, don't go falling back in love with it.

No ma'am.

I mean it, Wallace. You got a home to come back to.

You got it, he said.

I don't feel like you're listening to me, she said. I feel like maybe you're distracted.

Wallace told her quickly he wasn't, but he was lying. At that point he was standing in the parking lot of the Dairy Queen. Only it wasn't a Dairy Queen any more. Where there had once been a logo in the window, there was now clumsily written letters announcing it as the Thompson Family Diner. Instead of cones and hot dogs on the door there were black and white pictures of ugly looking platters of food.

You sure? Cindy said. You sound like your mind's elsewhere.

Sure as a heart attack, Wallace said. Honey, he said, I'm gonna get a bite to eat. You mind if I call you back?

You gonna call me back?

Sure, he said. In a few minutes.

Cause you say all the time you're gonna call back and then you don't.

Christ, he said. I said I'd call back, so I'll goddamn call back.

She went silent. He knew without a doubt she was pissed. That's what silence meant in her language.

Cindy, he said. I'm sorry.

It's fine, she said, her voice breaking with what sounded like oncoming tears. I'm just stressed out, here by myself.

Wallace kicked a rock on the ground and nodded. I know, he said, I know, I know, I know. I'm sorry that I'm way out here.

It's fine, she said. Go get something to eat.

I will, he said. And then I'm gonna call you right back. You hear me?

It's fine, she said. If you get busy, I understand.

I'll call, he said and then told her goodbye.

Inside, the restaurant looked almost identical to how it had once upon a time. The booths were still bright red, the counter set up in the exact same way the Dairy Queen had been, and there was still a big, wooden curly-cued cone on the wall by the freezer. But the menu by the cash register was different. Instead of hamburgers and hot dogs, there were pictures of beef stroganoff, spaghetti, slices of meatloaf and ham. A bored girl with plain brown hair pulled back in a lazy bun looked at Wallace as he walked in and barely raised an eye.

Welcome to Thompson's, she said.

He pointed at a booth and said, Do I sit or come to you?

You order up here, she said, then we bring it out.

Okay, he said and approached the register. The food looked awful on the menu, the lights coloring everything a sickly yellow hue. Thrown off, Wallace ordered a chicken fried steak with mashed potatoes and set himself down in one of the empty booths.

He'd been coming to the Dairy Queen since he was a little boy. It had been a tradition, after a peewee baseball game, to climb into his coach's truck and ride through town chanting We're number one, we're number one, until they'd pulled into the parking lot. On Sundays in the summer his mom and stepdad would take him there after church and he'd eat his ice cream as they walked from booth to booth, chatting and catching up on all of Bethel Baptist's newest gossip.

It'd been where he took Carol on their first date. Over shakes and fries they'd talked the better part of four hours until he looked up at the clock and realized she was an hour past curfew.

Here you go, the bored girl said and brought over his plate. It was Styrofoam and sagged at the edges from the food's heft. The steak was thin and resilient like a rubber shoe liner, and the mashed potatoes were drowning in a sea of pale gravy. He picked up the plastic knife and fork she'd given him and tried to cut the tough meat until the fork broke and he was forced to use his fingers to hold it steady.

He took his first bite and considered a second,

when music started to play over a speaker in the ceiling. When he turned to the register, he saw that the bored girl was messing with the dials on a banged-up radio. The song that played was an old one by *The Mamas & the Papas*. He hummed along to it and chewed on a piece of the steak. It wasn't the worst thing he'd ever eaten and definitely not the best.

After he swallowed he looked across the room at the booth by the window with the restaurant's name. That's where he and Carol had been. He remembered the way she'd looked at her watch and noticed the time and then launched herself in the direction of the payphone by the bathrooms to call her mother. Turning in his seat, Wallace glanced in that direction.

On the wall by the bathroom there was still a box where the payphone had been, but the phone itself was gone. All that remained was a hole in the wall and a few orphaned wires. Below it though was a phonebook, the cover and pages curling in on themselves like it'd been left out in the rain. There was a picture on the front of a mailbox on a dirt road.

The first page of the phonebook Wallace turned to was in the M's. Carol's maiden name was McKisson and he figured, if she hadn't gotten hitched again, she might be listed there. She wasn't though and neither were her folks. When the bell above the door to the restaurant chimed, Wallace turned in a hurry. His first thought was that Carp was coming in, that he somehow knew that Wallace was fumbling through the phonebook and was about to blow his head off. But it was an old couple, the two of them in sweatpants and sweatshirts, hobbling up to the counter.

Wallace turned to the W's. It didn't take long to come to WALLACE, CAROL and next to it his old address and a familiar number. Taking his phone out of his pocket, he searched through his contacts and came to the one labeled CAROL and checked that number against the one in the book. All the years, all the different phones, and he still always dialed their old number by memory.

He tore the page with Carol's number out of the phonebook, folded it, and shoved it deep into the pocket of his coat. A souvenir. When he got back to his booth the steak and potatoes were cold and a pool of grease and water had nearly congealed on the edges of the plate. He carried the plate over and dumped it into a trashcan. As he walked out, he saw that the old couple were sitting at a booth one over from the one he and Carol had shared so long ago. They were sitting there in silence, the old man twiddling his thumbs and the old woman searching through her purse for something, though Wallace didn't know what.

Chapter 9

The stray was barking in the street and, when Chief Dean woke, he recognized it immediately. Rat, as all the neighbors had taken to calling him, liked to follow the trash truck from stop to stop and harass the collectors. Climbing out of his sleep, Dean pulled the nearest curtain aside and watched Rat run circles around the truck while a worker named Charlie Bill dumped Dean's cans into the compactor.

Dean tossed back his covers and swung his legs over the side of the bed. Every morning was the same kind of misery. First he woke and then his knee squealed in pain. He looked at it, at the massive scar just off-center, at the star-shaped lump of white tissue. He thumped it like an old woman thumping a melon and felt a shock of pain rifle through his thigh.

Good morning, he said.

In the kitchen he cleaned out his coffee maker and lumped in enough Folgers to make six cups of coffee. In the morning he drank three cups, black, and poured the rest into his industrial-sized thermos. On the porch was that morning's paper. The headline was about the need for a new sewer system in town. In a sidebar next to it was an account of Jimmy Lee's arrest. The paper came out every other day, so the news had usually gone cold by the time it was delivered. The picture under the article was of Jimmy Lee back in the day, clad in a pair of kickboxing shorts

73

and standing over the fallen body of a rival. The caption read "THE HARDER THEY FALL James Lee Hardesty, former kickboxing hero of Seymour, was arrested for disorderly conduct by SPD at 11:35 pm in The Hideout bar."

Dean didn't bother reading any more of the account. He was used to the poor prose of the reporters and knew full and well there were probably some inaccuracies regarding the events. The coffee maker was gurgling and he got the cleanest mug he could find out of the sink in anticipation of his first cup.

Finished with his three cups and his thermos loaded, he got into his cruiser and putted down his dirt road and in the direction of town. Along the way was Fairview Cemetery. Regularly he stopped there on his way to work, choosing to pull in and go to the next to last section and visit with his mama. When he parked the cruiser and got out, the first thing he noticed were some objects on the grass directly in front of her grave.

When he got closer, he saw they were the empties from a six-pack of Bud Light, the bottles spread over the area, and on the base of the headstone itself a pair of spent rubbers. They looked like snake skins the way they were just laying there, baking in the sun. Dean surveyed the cemetery and saw that he was alone. He kicked the ground so hard he hurt his foot and covered his polished shoes with a coating of dust. He cursed the kids of Seymour, a generation of no accounts and idiots who, by his estimation, were getting worse every day.

Retrieving a pair of rubber gloves and an evidence bag from the trunk, he picked up the bottles and the rubbers and sealed the bag. Walking into the station, he found Bockwinkel with his legs up on his desk, watching a talk show on the nearby TV. He tossed the evidence bag on the desk and pointed at it.

Lookit that shit, he said. Lookit that goddamn shit.

Bockwinkel looked. Those condoms, Chief?

What the fuck you think they are? Dean said. Jellyfish?

Sorry Chief, Bockwinkel said and picked up the bag. He turned it this way and that. He squinted his eyes as if he were studying the contents. Where you find all this stuff? he said.

Dean put his fists on his hips. His anger hadn't subsided on his drive in. The more he thought about it, the more it pissed him off. That bullshit right there, he spit, was decorating my poor mama's grave.

Bockwinkel shook his head. That's just awful, Chief.

You better goddamn believe it's awful. There's a bunch of kids hanging out in Fairview getting drunk, and God knows what else, and fornicating all over the graves. You tell me how something like that happens. Just tell me.

Times are changing, Bockwinkel said. I know that much.

You and me both, Dean said. You know what my mama would've said about all this?

I reckon she would've said the End Times were coming.

I reckon she would've.

And you know what, Chief?

What's that?

I reckon she'd be right.

Me too, Dean said and carried the thermos over to his desk and set it down. When he got into his chair, he had a clear view into the cell where Jimmy Lee was sleeping and waiting for County to pick him up that afternoon and take him to his arraignment. Jimmy Lee, Dean yelled at him. Jimmy Lee, wake your good-for-nothing ass up.

Jimmy Lee rolled over and faced Dean, his eyes still half-closed. What's that? he said.

Jimmy Lee, Dean said, what do you make of a bunch of teenage shits getting drunk and fornicating all over my mama's grave?

Before he spoke Jimmy Lee shook his head like Bockwinkel had and then whistled through his teeth. He said, Chief, that's some cold-hearted shit.

That's what I'm thinking, Dean said, realizing all of a sudden that maybe he should let Jimmy Lee walk. That's just what he was thinking about the subject.

Chapter 10

Yorkie Goodman stepped out of his dirt-caked jeans and sweat-soaked shirt and walked through his house and into the bathroom. He reached down, turned on the hot water, and put his hand under the spray. It occurred to him that his life was nothing if not a sequence of repetitive tasks. Every day he turned on the water and every day he tested it in the same way and found himself shaking his hand off and waiting the same amount of time before he stepped in. He stepped in and rinsed off his body.

On the edge of the tub was a line of bars of Lava Soap. There were maybe eight of them and all in different states of use. Together they were like a miniature dilapidated stone wall. He picked the largest one and got to work lathering. The bar bit at his skin, a familiar feeling that he realized he had felt every day for the last twenty-five years.

After he dried off and dressed, he put on a white undershirt and a pair of jeans. He pulled on his town boots and grabbed his keys off the end table closest to the door. His old Chevy truck chewed up oil, so he popped the hood before he left and dropped in a quart for the road. After a couple of cranks, the truck came alive and he rumbled down the dirt road and onto the gravel. First he passed by Fairview Cemetery and then, a ways down, the elementary school. Children were out for recess, chasing each other through the grass and playing basketball on the far away courts. Like he always did, Yorkie beeped his horn and watched some of the children snap their heads to attention and then wave as he drove by.

At Thompson's Family Diner he walked up to the register and Melanie Thompson, the wife of the owner, smiled and handed him the sweet tea she had waiting on him. You want your regular? she asked him.

Sure, he said. Why not? Maybe a little bit of pepper too?

Sure thing, she said, and he went to his usual booth by the freezer. There were a few pages of the paper spread around on the table and he rifled through them, glancing at stories he'd already read. Not long after, Melanie brought him a Styrofoam plate stuffed with a mountain of noodles and mashed potatoes, and littered with specks of pepper. That enough for you? she asked.

I reckon so, he said with a nod.

He ate his lunch and then dropped the empty plate into the trashcan by the door. As he walked out, a van from the nursing home had just pulled up outside and a couple of nurses were helping the old folks step off, holding their arms and telling them to take the next step easy, take it easy.

Afternoon, Yorkie said as he walked by them.

His next stop was the Sur-Way, a grocery store out by the AutoZone. This time of day there was nobody there save for the people working the registers and shelves and the blue-hairs who took two or more hours to get their groceries. Yorkie zipped by them and picked up everything he needed, the same items he'd been buying regularly for God knows how long. A loaf of Bunny Bread, dozen eggs, gallon of whole milk, a pack of cold fried chicken from the deli, and another bar of Lava Soap. The girl at the register had a ring in her nose and, while she checked him out, he stared at it and wondered just how much force it would take to rip it right out and hold it in his hand. He decided, as she gave him his receipt, it wouldn't be much.

Across the street, tucked back behind the ice plant, was a little brick building with a green and white sign that said In-And-Out. Yorkie went straight for the cooler directly opposite the front door and grabbed a six-pack of Busch Light and carried it up to the register. The boy behind it was named Seth and, though Yorkie never brought it up, he'd gone to school with Seth's granddad, a fella named Roland that everybody called Slip. Every so often Yorkie thought about mentioning it to the kid and telling him about the time that Slip, who was a hell of a runner in his heyday, won County by close to ten yards. It'd been all anyone talked about for years. Every time Yorkie didn't tell Seth about it, he'd get in his truck, set the six-pack on the seat next to him, and sit there and cuss himself for not telling the boy.

Forgetting about it a few seconds later, Yorkie got on the road. As he did he popped open the pack of cold fried chicken and ate a drumstick down to the bone. When he was done, he rolled down his window and tossed it into a passing ditch. It had tasted pretty good, so he got out another and made quick work out of it too.

It was five after four when he cracked open the first beer. He did it as he looked at the clock on his stove. The time was off by twenty-five minutes. He knew that but never gave serious thought to fixing it. He thought about his son Mike and how he was probably finishing up his shift for the day at the electric company and that he'd give him a couple of minutes to get out of there and maybe give him a ring.

To fill his time he stepped into the living room and clicked on the TV. There wasn't anything good on, so he settled for a show where doctors came on and told him what was healthy and what wasn't. He hated that show, but he always found himself watching it and yelling back at the screen, I'm sixty-one years old and I made it this goddamn far without being told what to eat. To punctuate his point he grabbed another beer off the ring and slugged it down.

All right, the doctor said on the TV, let's talk about pork.

Yorkie found himself laughing like he'd just heard the funniest joke in the world and picked up his cordless phone. He dialed Mike's cell and when he picked up he said, There's a doctor on the TV right now telling me what he thinks about pork. What do you think about pork, Mike?

It's all right in my book, Mike said. Never done wrong by me.

That's what I think, Yorkie said. Hey, he said, how's business, son?

Yorkie and his son talked for twenty minutes about what the company had Mike doing and how his family and kids were and how Illinois was treating him. All that Yorkie talked about were his soybeans and how he was hoping for some rain sooner or later but wasn't holding out hope.

All right dad, Mike told him at the end, talk to you later.

You too, son, Yorkie said.

He put the phone back and pulled another beer off the ring. The doctor was showing a picture of a cartoon pig and the pig had great big eyes and a smile a mile wide. There were dotted lines all along his body and the sections were labeled for their cuts of meat. To Yorkie it was the damnedest thing he ever saw. He raised pigs and knew they were disgusting creatures that wallowed in their own shit and would eat anything put in front of them.

The show made him hungry and he went into the kitchen and got a can of Spam out of the cabinet and sat back down in front of the TV with it and listened to the doctor go on and on about heart disease and cholesterol and all that good stuff. He drank his third beer and got to work on his fourth. Outside it was starting to get dark, so he put down the can and started turning on the lights in the house. Every night he turned on the same five lights, even though there were close to two-dozen in the house. When he was done, the living room where he sat was sparsely lit and the light under the stove's hood in the kitchen was on. He sat back down, had a drink of beer, and then took a bite of the Spam.

The doctor show was over a little while later and the news came on. The anchors were talking about some festival going on in Indianapolis and Yorkie only paid half attention to what they had to say. The next beer was opened and he finished off the Spam and tossed the beer can into the kitchen to be picked up later. The footage on the news was of some people standing behind a table and selling raffle tickets. He was looking at them handing out tickets and the way they looked so nervous being watched by the TV camera, when he thought he saw something move outside.

He stood up and went to the window. It wasn't completely dark but dark enough that he had a hard time making out his own yard. There were trees and a tractor he hadn't messed with in years and left to rust. He looked at the bushes he needed to trim and decided it was probably nothing but a rabbit, maybe a fawn that was too young to know any better. He sat down again and watched the weather forecast until he decided it was time for another beer.

Chapter 11

Boss and Abel waited in the back of the Range Rover, Abel playing a game on his phone while Boss listened halfheartedly to a talk show on the radio. We're looking at a major realignment, the host said. These people we've given the keys to, they're not like us. They come from a background of socialist ideas and radical philosophies. If you ask me, every morning I wake up now it's like I'm waking up to a whole different country.

I think, Boss said to Abel, you'd do well to put that phone away.

One second, Abel said and continued mashing at the touchscreen.

Boss looked out the window at the building. A few of the lights were still on but the OPEN sign had long since been shut off. Through the glass he could see shapes moving around inside. Boss picked his own phone out of his pocket and looked at the screen. No calls, no messages. He wondered what Carp and Wallace were up to in Indiana.

That's some bullshit, Abel said to his phone.

In one quick motion Boss grabbed Abel's phone and tossed it into the front seat. It hit the floor with a thud and the screen went black.

What the hell? Abel said.

I told you, Boss said. Told you to put the phone away.

Abel crossed his chest with his arms and sulked. You don't have to be such a prick about it.

Boss thought to himself, Yes, I do, and then saw movement in his periphery. Simmons was approaching the car, looking both ways on the street. When Boss rolled down the window, he nodded and said, Inside's secure. No one's gonna bother you in there.

Good, Boss said and motioned for Abel to step out of the car. The two of them walked across the street and into the building, a bell above the door jingling as they did and the smell of wood and dust hitting them smack in the face. The antique store wasn't particularly well organized, or well kept, but from an initial scan Boss could see the inventory was numerous and impressive. The owner was seated behind a desk, his fingers knotted together, his gaze bent down on them. Evening, Boss said to him.

Without looking up the owner said, Evening. And then, when he saw Boss, I'm sorry. I'm really, really sorry.

Boss sucked on his bottom lip and turned to Abel. This is what happens, he said. You confront someone about their transgressions and inevitably they're gonna tell you they're sorry.

No, the owner said, looking up, his eyes wet with forming tears, I mean it. I got screwed by a dealer in New Orleans. That's the God's honest truth.

Next, Boss said to Abel, they'll pass the buck. It's not their fault. It's somebody else's fault. Maybe it's everyone else's fault. Most motherfuckers would give up their grandmas if it meant living another hour.

The owner returned to leaning his head on his hands and his shoulders bounced as he began to sob.

Come over here, Boss said to him.

For a moment the owner resisted. He mumbled, I don't want to.

I said, Boss said, get the fuck over here.

At Boss' command the owner stood from his stool and dragged his feet all the way over to where Boss and Abel were standing. A piece of furniture in the back of the store shifted, the noise causing the owner to jump. I'm sorry, he said after he'd regained his composure. I'm just so sorry.

Abel turned away from the owner and his crying, but Boss grabbed him and forced him to look. I don't want to look at him, Abel whispered.

You have to, Boss said. Abel, this man right here, this piece of shit, he insulted your mother. And when he insulted your mother, he insulted me. And do you know who else he insulted?

Who? Abel said.

You, Boss said.

Listen, the owner said, I didn't mean to insult anybody. The way this business works, I swear, sometimes things don't come in on time.

Boss crossed the distance between them and sent the owner to the floor with a backhand. When he looked up at Boss and Abel, his lip was busted and a bruise was starting to birth on his cheek. He looked sick now.

I'm gonna ask you to shut your mouth, Boss said. I'm teaching my son here.

Leave him alone, Abel said.

Abel, Boss said, if you know what's good for you, son, you'll shut your mouth too and listen.

With a huff Abel shifted to his back foot like he was about to leave.

Don't you dare, Boss said. Don't you fucking dare.

You can take whatever you want, the owner said. I mean it, no charge. Call it even.

Boss grabbed the owner by the lapels of his shirt and snapped him up to his feet and dragged him over to the desk he'd been sitting behind. He slammed his head down onto the desk and the sound of flesh and bone meeting wood, like a wet rag being thrown into a wall, sent a shock of nausea straight into Abel's gut.

Son, Boss said to him, get over here.

Abel didn't move. He was too busy trying not to throw up.

With one hand Boss held the owner down as he gagged and cried and with the other he beckoned Abel to join him. The boy did with trepidation and Boss reached into a pocket in his coat and produced a snub-nose with a taped-over grip. When Abel didn't immediately take it, Boss screamed at him, Be a fucking man and take the fucking gun.

Abel took the gun. It was the first time he'd ever held one. He felt its heft, the strange power it contained, the ability to take life without any consideration.

Put it to this worthless sonuvabitch's head, Boss said. Then, No, not there, higher, right above the knot.

Abel leveled the gun, aiming it a few inches higher than he was told.

The owner screamed and Boss bucked his knee up

and into his gut. At first he nearly buckled and then, after Boss steadied him, he began making a noise that vibrated out of his mouth like the bleating of a sheep.

Cock the hammer, Boss told Abel. After he did, Boss told him to pull the trigger, but Abel hesitated again. Abel, he said, his voice calm and level, I know this is the hardest part. Always is. It gets easier though. I promise.

I can't, Abel said, his hand starting to shake.

Absolutely you can, Boss said.

The owner bleated louder and louder.

Animals kill, Boss said. We're animals, son. We're the most goddamn magnificent animals walking around on two feet. We built the goddamn railroad. We conquered the continents and swam all the oceans and landed on the motherfucking moon. Least you can do is squeeze that little trigger and put this piece of shit out of his misery.

Abel did as he was told and as soon as he did he was struck by how easy it had been. The owner had been struggling right there on the desk one second and lay in a bloody heap the next. It was as simple as a little pressure.

You feel good? Boss said.

I feel all right, Abel said.

Good boy, Boss said and took the snub-nose and replaced it in his coat. Tell you what, he said, slugging his arm around Abel's shoulder and leading him into the heart of the store, let's pick out something nice for Mom. Just you and me. How about that?

Chapter 12

There was only a brief line of sight through the rows of corn but Chief Dean could make out a sliver of Fairview Cemetery across the road. He'd parked in Yorkie Goodman's second field, kept company by his thermos of coffee, a bag of salt and vinegar chips, and a radio program turned down to a whisper. It was an old show from the Fifties and two kids were talking to each other about going on an adventure in the most unnatural of voices.

What do you think, Merle? one of them said.

I think, Dean said between mouthfuls of chips, here before too long there ain't gonna be many Merle's left. The vinegar made his jaw hurt and he tried to help the situation with a swig of coffee. After swallowing, he rolled down his window, smelled the fall air, and looked across the street, hoping to see a shadow of movement at last.

In his training he'd been taught how to sight through even the darkest of evenings. Focus on the stillness, the instructor had told him. Nothing is its own kind of something. Watch for that nothing to be upset.

He trained on the dark again and waited for movement, for some dumbass kid to trip up and stumble through his field of vision. The plan was half-baked. He was gonna stakeout the cemetery for however long it took, the next ten years if it came to that, and catch those bastards in the act. He owed that to his mama, he'd told himself. After all she'd done, all she'd sacrificed, all she'd given him, it was the least he could do.

Dean thought of how the whole thing would go down. He was going to see those kids, drunk and high off their asses, and he was gonna gun the engine and burst out of that field like a house a fire and whip into the cemetery's closest drive. Those kids would probably be fumbling to get in their cars and he'd roll up with his lights blazing and his gun drawn. He could see it clear as day, their faces as he got them on the ground and cuffed them so hard it cut into their skin. After that, he'd decided, he was gonna drag them over to his mama's grave and get 'em down in the grass and tell 'em it was time to start apologizing.

Thinking about that made Dean grin from ear to ear. Those kids' whining was gonna be music to him and it made the wait that much more bearable. That was good because he hadn't been on a stakeout in fourteen years, since the SPD got word that Terry Wilcox had taken up hiding in his grandma's house with an arsenal. That'd been one for the books.

Wilcox was a sadistic sonuvabitch who'd gotten all the breaks. Years before he'd broken into the house of an old man by the name of Saul Weatherspoon and robbed him blind. But that hadn't been enough. No, sir. Wilcox'd gone back and beat the living hell out of Weatherspoon with a tire iron for what seemed like no reason. Even said as much in questioning. But one of the officers on the case, an old friend of Dean's named Brinson, had seized some of the evidence without proper authorization and left the report full of holes. Wilcox walked.

Luckier than shit, Dean said to himself in his car.

The next time, Wilcox was having a dispute with the mother of his baby girl. Went over there, told her he was gonna burn her house down, and then sloshed a can of gas on her front porch and lit a match. There must've been two-dozen witnesses in the neighborhood, but when Dean went to ask, they told him they hadn't seen anything. No matter what he told them, no matter how much he promised he could protect them, no one was willing to say anything bad about Wilcox. He was mean, legendarily so, and nobody, not even the mother of the child he tried to burn to death, wanted to cross him.

But that kind of luck had a way of corrupting. Dean knew that. He'd seen low-lifes in the past who got so drunk on their own providence they didn't know where the line was. Didn't know where to stop. And Wilcox was no different. The way the story went was this – he'd been drinking at Hilliard's with a bunch of buddies from the lumberyard he worked at and took a liking to one of the waitresses there. Christie Wallace. She'd been a pretty girl, nineteen years of age, and a lot of the boys who went in there took a liking to her. Most of them whistled or asked her out, while some of them fought and caused a scene. Wilcox though, he didn't mess with any of that. He just waited out her shift, followed her through the door, and got her pinned down on the sidewalk outside.

It had been such a blatant and awful crime that

even his good ol' pals in Hilliard's served as witnesses. A few ran out there to help Christie but Wilcox pulled a Bowie knife out of the side of his boot and kept the would-be rescuers at a distance. When he was done, he got up and walked away like he hadn't ever considered doing a thing wrong.

Of course, there were more than enough people watching to get him arrested. There were even cameras on the bank drive-thru across the street. All in all, it was an open and shut case. The easiest of Dean's career, that was for sure. And Dean was gonna love the hell out of seeing Wilcox get his. When he got word that he'd shown up at his grandma's house, after going missing the better part of a week, Dean jumped in his cruiser, bringing along his rifle and scope for good measure, and got there before anyone else.

Fourteen hours. That's how long Wilcox held out. The next morning he came out, laid a sawed-off on the steps leading in, and asked if anybody had any food. Within the hour he was in the jail and chewing on a hamburger.

That afternoon Dean had been filling out some of the paperwork on Wilcox, when Bill Wallace, a good-for-nothing in his own right, strolled into the office with a Glock in hand. Dean was slow to react and hadn't gotten out from behind his desk before Wallace had fired the first of a pair of shots into Wilcox's forehead. His first instinct had been to unholster himself and let Wallace have it – he knew now, in his car, his knee aching like a bastard, that he should've done just that – but he felt bad for Bill, for Christie, for everybody, and wanted to try and calm the situation before it got any worse. A few steps in Bill turned and Dean saw the look on his face. He wasn't gonna kill him, he knew that, but he wasn't gonna give up either. The gun swung his way. He saw the flash and felt a world of fire and pain enter his knee.

On the floor he'd been writhing and screaming as Bill walked out of the office. Bit down so hard on his lip that he chewed through his bottom one and unlocked a mouthful of blood for his trouble. The knee felt like it had come apart, disintegrated into a cloud of bone and tissue and then come back together with a wave of heat. It was as if a miniature sun had exploded into life in the wound and was waking up and stretching its arms into the meat of his leg and then the rest of his body.

Thinking about that made Dean jumpy. Every day since, he'd had at least one moment where he relived that, where he felt the pain all over again. If Bill Wallace had been sitting there in the passenger seat, right then, Dean would've pulled his piece and splattered his brains on the window. My God it hurt, even now, fourteen years later.

Fourteen years, Dean thought to himself and then whistled. Fourteen years.

That got him thinking of those fourteen years and all that they'd brought.

Wars.

Crime.

A handful of murders.

And then the thing he was trying not to think about, trying not to say. Mama's death. Her lying strapped to a bed, withering away for eight months to the tune of a crowd of machines and the beat of who knows how many nurses walking in and walking out of her cold little room at St. Methodist.

Mama, Dean thought, snapping his attention back to his stakeout and to the clearing through the corn just in time to see the nothing being disturbed.

He threw open his door, forgetting all about his plans to run the kids down, choosing instead to rush out of his car and across the road. He could hear the sound of two people running across the cemetery and he knew, as sure as he knew the immediate pain in his knee, that he'd made a mistake in ditching his car, as he stood no chance in hell of catching up with them. Instead, he pulled out his flashlight and directed the beam in their direction.

The pair, in his estimation, looked larger than a couple of kids out for some horsing around. And from his brief glimpse, they were dressed head to toe in black and wearing ski masks to boot.

Dean watched them disappear over a distant hill and heard, not long after, the sound of an engine coming to life. His first instinct was to get his cruiser and track them down, but something gave him pause. The voice in his head, the one that'd served well to keep him out of the worst jambs, spoke to him, loudly and matter-of-factly, Dean, you old shit, leave well enough alone.

Sure enough, Dean said to himself and then walked a few rows over to his mama's grave. He clicked on the flashlight again and saw it was undisturbed save for a few stray leaves. Next he looked out into the neighboring thatch of trees that separated Fairview from Yorkie Goodman's property. He focused the light on the hedgerow and saw where part of a rusted wire fence had been cut and tossed aside.

He was about to go and get a closer look, when that voice started talking again. All right, he said, tipping his cap at the grave, guess I'm going home. Night, Mama, he said and headed for his car.

Chapter 13

Back at the motel Carp was stripping off his black shirt and pants while Wallace tore the room apart. I'm telling you, he said, I can't find that piece of shit. Doesn't matter where I look.

Have you checked your pockets? Carp said.

Of course I've checked my pockets, Wallace said. What do you think I am? Some kind of fucking idiot? The goddamn thing's missing.

Carp shook his head. I'm beginning to worry about your competence.

I'm very competent. I'm just about the most competent motherfucker you ever met. This isn't about competency. This is about dumb luck.

We'll agree to disagree.

I'm telling you, Wallace said, it must've fallen out of the car when we got out.

That's highly unlikely. Carp was down to his skin and lying on top of his bed, his body straight as a board and his eyes focused again on the ceiling. Wallace looked at him and how pale he was, pale, he thought, as a can of white paint. Chances are, Carp said, clasping his hands on his chest, you misplaced it among your things.

Wallace grabbed handfuls of his clothes and tossed them into the air. Does it look like it's among my things, Carp? Sure as shit that thing fell out of the car.

Then we'll go back and look.

No, Wallace said. That's fine. I'll go. No need to waste your time.

Carp had already sat back up and was reaching for his pants. That's fine, he said. Better that we go together.

Nah, Wallace said. Don't worry about it. I'll go. I'll run and make quick work out of it. Sides, chances are there's a call out about two guys running around out there. Whoever that was with the flashlight probably called it in. Better that only one of us goes.

Then I'll go, Carp said. You're wanted in this area.

Carp, Wallace said, I'm going. It's my wallet. It's my mistake.

With another shake of the head, Carp relented and laid back down. You're behaving suspiciously, Wallace. Like somebody with something to hide.

I'm not saying this again, Wallace said, grabbing the keys off the table by the door, there's nothing suspicious. I lost my wallet. Last thing we need to do is leave behind something to ID us. Lay the fuck off.

Carp sucked in a long stream of air and Wallace watched his chest balloon in size until he released it through his nose. I'll be expecting you back shortly, he said finally.

Wallace chose not to respond and went out to the car. As he reached for the door handle, he checked with his other hand just to make sure his wallet was secure in his back pocket. After pulling out and onto the highway he turned down an old back road, one that he and his buddies had used whenever they'd drunk too much and wanted to avoid the police, a maze they'd taken to calling the Second Highway. It wormed its way through a couple of trailer parks and eventually out by the VFW. After a stretch of dilapidated horse barns and RV stops, he ended up on Walleye Street, which turned, after a couple of miles, into Rural Route 3.

If he'd wanted to, Wallace could've turned off the headlights and made it to the house without so much as a second thought. The timing of the drive, the bumps and contours of the road, were still second nature, even after fourteen years. A few of the houses had been painted, some trees planted and some fallen, but as far as he could see in the dark that stretch was just as it'd been the day he'd gotten into his truck, driven to the station, and shot Terry Wilcox in his worthless fucking head.

The mailbox out on the road was even the same. A red one with the name WALLACE on the side. He slowed the car to a near halt next to it and marveled at its continued existence. Carol's dedication, even from afar, humbled him. For months on end he'd kept an eye on the Seymour newspaper online just to see what they said about him shooting Wilcox and that deputy. And he'd never been able to keep himself from checking the wedding announcements and marriage licenses. Truth be told, he wouldn't of blamed her for finding another man, which would've been easy enough considering how goddamn beautiful and kind Carol was, but part of him hated that he put himself through that kind of torture. And here she was, still walking out to get the mail every single day, looking at that name on the side of the mailbox, the name of a man who'd been gone over a decade, who'd left her high and dry and fled for greener pastures.

Before he rolled the car down the small gravel driveway that led into the house, he cut the lights and the motor. He didn't want to scare Carol, primarily because he remembered, down to the serial numbers, the collection of guns he'd left behind. Carol hadn't been one to shoot them with any regularity or accuracy, but he knew that, if he woke her and gave her enough time, she'd reach for his granddad's twelve-gauge and he knew that didn't take any kind of practice or any kind of accuracy to do some harm.

The home itself was an old farm house built in the early 1870's, a blue-sided box sitting in front of a field of dirt too stubborn to grow any manner of crops, regardless of seed or attention given. It had belonged to Wallace's great-great granddad, Theodore Wallace, a hobby farmer who'd never made a dime. From there, down to Wallace himself, the house had passed from hand-to-hand until he'd abandoned it and Carol alongside.

The steps groaned in a familiar way as he climbed up to the door. The windows were black, meaning Carol was in bed. She'd always been of two minds when it came to rest. She was either out hard – so hard that she once slept through a six-shot volley in which Wallace had dispatched a thug from Indianapolis named Denton in the living room – or else crawling nervously through the house at all hours, the lights juiced up in an effort to combat the night terrors she got every few months.

Those terrors were something. Screaming,

shrieking episodes where Carol launched herself from under the sheets and went room to room, crying and carrying on like the end was nigh.

Wallace shook his head while thinking about it and pulled his keys out of his pocket. On the outside chance it would work, he selected the key he'd had since he was a kid and slid it into the lock. It worked with a delightful click, the house saying, he thought, Welcome home.

Inside he studied the shadow-heavy walls. Portraits in the same place. Pictures of him, Christie, Carol and him, his step-dad, his mom. A framed picture he'd bought her one Mother's Day – a cartoon woman slaving over a stove, a smile stretching across her face, the words A FAMILY'S WORK IS NEVER DONE underlining the image.

He didn't bother hiding the sound of his boots as he walked to the bedroom. If Carol was going to come out with the twelve-gauge, it would've happened already. Instead, he found her in bed the way he always had: covers thrown madly to the side, her body contorted, mouth open as if about to ask a question.

Sitting on the side of the bed, he touched her hair. She was older, sure, but familiar still, comfortable the same way the house was. No, he thought, beautiful. Home, he thought.

Carol, he whispered. Carol, baby.

She rolled and slung her arm just past his knee. With a groan she said, Honey.

Honey, he said. Baby. He stroked her hair, her face. I need you to wake up.

Instantly her eyes opened like a pair of curtains

being flung back. She was up on her knees, her face already contorted in shock.

Calm down, Wallace said, and reached out to touch her. I'm going to explain, but you have to calm down.

Carol was quick to shrug off his touch and rolled out of the other side of the bed. In a long T-shirt and nothing else she scrambled in the dark toward the closet. Wallace knew that's where the shotgun was. It's where he'd kept it all those years.

Carol, he said, Jesus. You need to calm down, honey.

She didn't listen, instead flinging open the closet and grabbing the shotgun, cocking the hammers as she scurried into the nearest corner. She was talking, saying a slurry of words, but Wallace could barely make out anything particular.

He was terrified that she might fire both barrels and reduce him to a cloud of blood and bone. But then it dawned on him that Carol, waking up so suddenly, believed she was in the grip of one of her night terrors.

Carol, he said. I'm real.

No, she said.

He could see the barrels shaking.

Yes, he said. I'm back.

Carol uncocked the hammers. As soon as she did, Wallace rushed across the room and snatched the shotgun from her hands. He ejected both slugs and laid it on the bed.

Where? Carol managed to choke out. She was crying, hard, her hands covering her face. The words continued to pour, each one running into the next.

Thought you were ... dead ... thought ...

I'm not, he said and lowered himself next to her. When he first tried to hold her, she fought, but relented when he gave it one more try. I'm alive, he said and moved her hands to his face. I'm alive, he said again, and then, I'm sorry.

For a while he held her, felt her shaking and sobbing and heaving into his shoulder. It had been so long since he'd touched her, felt her, smelled her. It was like he'd been in a dream until that moment.

So engrossed in the moment he forgot what he'd come for. He was reminded though when he heard a car pass on the road and thought of Carp. The sound sent a jolt through him and he held Carol at a distance and met her eyes with his own.

I'll explain everything, he promised, but I don't have long right now.

Y ... you, she stammered.

Carol, he said. I need you to tell me. Do you want to be with me or do you want me to disappear again?

At that she squalled like an upset baby, her features scrunching and her mouth opening in a terrible rictus. Why? she screamed. You're so cruel, she screamed.

Carol, he said. Baby. I need you to focus. I'll explain everything, I promise. And we can be together. Tell me you understand. I need you to tell me you understand that.

We can, she said, the tears still sliding down her face, be together.

That's right, he said. Do you still have a key to your grandpa's cabin? The one in Brown County?

Carol's mouth closed and finally some calm returned. Suddenly she seemed angry though, near violence. Yes, she managed.

If you want to be with me, he said, we're going to have to stay there awhile. We're gonna have to lay low. You hear me?

Why? she said. Why should I want to be with you anymore? You left. You left fourteen years ago, she said and slapped him hard across the face. Fourteen fucking years.

Sure, Wallace said, rubbing the place on his cheek as he stood up from the floor. I've got to go, honey.

I hate you, she said, and slunk in the corner. Then, off-handedly, What do you need?

Well, he said, looking around and feeling momentarily lost, I need you to get up tomorrow and buy enough supplies for a month. Make that a month and a half. I'll join you at the cabin the day after probably.

Carol nodded. She was looking down at her feet. Anything else? she said.

Wallace looked back at the bed and the twelve-gauge. Yeah, he said. Bring the shotgun. And one of my rifles.

She nodded in an absent way, in a manner that told Wallace she was still sore about the whole thing. I hope I can forgive you, she said, her body shaking.

Just get the things, Wallace said and made for the door. We'll get to that.

I mean, she said, running a finger down the length of one leg, I hope I can forgive you somehow.

You and me both, he said.

Chapter 14

Boss lay on top of the covers and listened to his heartbeat. He had just finished making love to his wife, a physical session that saw the two of them christening the surfaces of her newest bedroom pieces. Afterward she'd gone quickly to sleep and left him to sit and wonder if the next beat was going to be his last. For most of his life he'd been terrified of that organ, a pulsing piece of meat in his chest that seemed destined to burst. He felt it punching at him and tried to calm it with his thoughts.

Easy now, he thought. Easy, easy, easy.

He ran his hand up and down his sweaty chest and then wiped it off on the sheet. In that moment he felt as if he were minutes away from death.

His phone, in the pocket of the sport jacket she'd ripped off of him when she'd seen the new bedroom furniture, buzzed on the floor. Boss thought twice about rolling over to answer. Movement, no matter how slight, seemed like a bad idea when staving off a heart attack. But he knew who was on the other end, so he made the effort and hit the answer button.

Carp, he said without looking at the screen. Tell me how it goes.

Reconnaissance was fine, Carp said flatly. Wallace is gone with the car now. I suspect he's gone to make contact with his wife.

You're probably right, Boss said and swung his

legs over the side. His feet hit the floor and he looked across the room at the new full-length mirror. Even in the dark he could see the reflection of his large body slumped over. You think he'll be back?

Fifty-fifty, Carp said.

All right. If he comes back, you play it on the level until he gets ready to split.

Fine, Carp said.

And if he doesn't, you take care of the target and then go looking.

Fine, Carp said.

Boss looked at his reflection again and with his free hand he lifted up a roll of fat and watched it fall. How's Yorkie look? he said.

Old, Carp said. Vulnerable.

Good, Boss said. You have any questions?

No, sir. Just making contact as prescribed.

Keep me updated, he said and clicked the button to end the call. Before he laid back down he dropped the phone back onto his coat and looked at the mirror. The man staring back was someone he hadn't recognized in a very long time. He gave up trying and got back in bed. His wife was still sleeping, her slim and curvy body rising quietly and falling. He placed his hand on her ribs and felt the motion, the give and the take. He closed his eyes and kept it there, bargaining with his heart and trying his hardest to make its beat fall in line with hers.

Chapter 15

All that were left in the way of animals on Yorkie Goodman's farm were a pair of sows he'd taken to calling Tweedle-Dee and Tweedle-Dumb. Tweedle-Dee, the older, was a spotted Yorkshire plagued with a terrible set of nerves. When she got too stressed – which was often – she'd rub her sides against the boards of her small pen until she'd worn layers of her skin off and left behind raw wounds. Tweedle-Dumb, the larger of the two, rarely moved at all except for when Yorkie came to sling feed in the morning.

There you go, Yorkie said, tossing a handful in their trough while watching Tweedle-Dum raise herself from their nest and come barreling over. 'Nough for everybody, now. 'Nough for everybody.

Yorkie liked to stand by the pen and watch the pair eat their way through a pile of grubs, corn, and rotten apples. The sound of their chewing, though wet and punctuated with snorts and gagging when they got greedy, was comforting to him. It reminded Yorkie of his wife Janice and how, in her last days, she used to bring a cup of coffee out to him and then stand there watching the girls eat their breakfast.

I wish, she'd said nearly every morning, that Tweedle-Dee could get to feeling better.

She's fine, Yorkie would tell her between sips. She's just working things out.

Janice would just nod and say, Aren't we all?

He would've been content to stand there remembering, except the sound of a car driving down his driveway caught his attention. He looked to see a police cruiser sending up a cloud of dust. It stopped ten yards away and Chief Dean stepped out. He had on a heavy coat and looked to Yorkie to be running on a few sleepless nights.

Morning, Chief, Yorkie said.

Morning, Dean said and shook Yorkie's hand. He pointed at the sows and said, Looks like you got you a herd there.

You betcha. Almost too much to keep up with.

I bet. Sorry to take up your time, Yorkie, but I was gonna ask if you've noticed anything missing last couple of days.

Missing?

Maybe some anhydrous?

Yorkie reached into his overalls and scratched his chest. He turned his head and looked in the direction of his barn. Not that I know of.

All right, Dean said. Needed to check in. I was doing some work over by Fairview last night and saw a couple of fellas cutting across. Thought maybe they were creeping round here.

Shitfire, Yorkie said. Can't say anything's come up missing.

It's a damned shame ain't it?

That's exactly what it is, Chief. These druggies ain't got the sense God gave 'em.

You can say that again. We knock down two or three a month. Somehow they just keep popping up.

I read all 'bout it in the papers. Just makes you

sick.

Sure does, Dean said. You wouldn't believe the kind of shitholes these people are living in. Kids, dogs, you name it. Trash everywhere. People coming all hours of the night. I got stories I could tell you, I tell you that.

I doubt I'd want to hear 'em, Chief.

You bet your ass you wouldn't, Dean said and hustled himself. These people, they're animals. Worse than these here pigs, that's for sure. They get in an RV, a pick-up with a top on the back, and they cruise around while they're mixing their shit up. Half the time they hit a bump and blow themselves to kingdom come. You talk about a mess.

I heard something about that on the news, Yorkie said, remembering a story on the Indianapolis station. A couple had been on a back road, the woman driving a truck and the fella in a trailer hooked onto the back. Something had gone wrong with the cook and the whole trailer liked to have blown up. Course, that spooked the lady and she jackknifed the truck, sending the trailer flying into a nearby park to tumble around like a half-crazed fireball.

Well, Dean said, I ain't gonna bug you too long.

You sure I can't hustle you for a cup of coffee? Yorkie said. Ain't a problem.

Huh. You know, I could be convinced.

Let me rinse off my hands, Yorkie said. You go on in and make yourself at home.

Dean climbed the concrete steps up to Yorkie's back door, his knee barking the whole way. Inside he was first aware of a sour smell, the scent of mold and rot. Dishes and empty beer cans were piled on the counters, bowls half-full of milk spoiling on the kitchen table. Dean took a seat there and nudged one of them as far away as he could manage.

The home looked a lot like his had once upon a time. Back after he and a woman named Eliza had split. She was a music teacher at the high school, the one and only woman Dean had ever dared to love besides his mother.

Thinking about her made him take a deep draw of breath in through his nose and then out his mouth. He'd taken the end of things hard – he loved his work too much, she said, brought it home and slept on it like a pillow – and afterward his house had fallen into disrepair.

Trash climbing out of its can.

Dust coating everything in sight.

Bed sheets so overdue for a change that they started stinking like the booze he sweated out every night.

Dean was relieved when Yorkie came in, happy to not have to think anymore.

Chief, he said, you didn't get you a cup.

Hell if I did. Got in here and forgot what I was up to.

Story of my life, Yorkie said before he went and pulled a couple of mugs out of the heap of dishes. He gave them a quick rinse and filled them to the top. Dean watched a slosh of the stuff run over and drip down Yorkie's knuckles.

Thank ya, he said, taking his cup.

Yorkie sat down across from him and worked a

tooth over with his tongue. You know, he said, I think you might be the first person 'sides myself in this place in five years.

That right?

Since the old lady passed I ain't much for socializin'.

Know the feeling, Dean said. He was about to say more but something halted him. Instead he took a drink. The hot coffee burned his tongue. He knew then he'd rather not be here, anywhere else for that matter, and he sure as hell didn't want to talk about Yorkie's wife. Despite knowing the coffee was too hot, he took another pull so he could finish as fast as possible.

I don't know, Yorkie said to break the silence.

Dean agreed. Me either.

Yorkie moved his tongue to the other side of his mouth before saying, Say, what was you doing out this way last night anyhow?

Oh, hell, Dean said. I went out to visit Mama's grave the other day.

How long she been gone, Chief?

Seven years. Round that long.

She was a good woman, Yorkie said. Always did me and mine right.

She was one of God's very best, Dean said, realizing he was using one of his mama's favorite phrases. That woman would of done anything for anybody.

I know that.

That's what like to piss me off, Dean said and took another mouthful of coffee. Went out there and saw

111

where some kids had been messing around by her grave.

Yorkie's tongue stopped and he set his cup down to lean in and point at Dean. That? he said. That right there is what I'm talking about. He quit pointing and went back to his cup, but he continued, saying, There ain't a bit of good left, Chief. Say and do what you want 'bout the living, but always seemed to me you treat the dead with some respect.

Exactly. You just damn near put your finger on it.

What the hell is this place turnin' into? Yorkie said. I was watching a show the other day about this funeral home in Virginia, I think it was.

That the one where they were cremating so much they lost track of whose ashes was whose?

That's the one.

Goddamn.

They said they were piling bodies on top of each other. Chief, you're a man of the law, where the hell is the decency anymore? Just where has it gone? That's what I want to know.

You and me both, Dean said, almost done with his coffee. He looked down to see the last splash circling the bottom. Somebody like that, he said, somebody like Mama, they ought to have a statue out in front of City Hall.

You bet she should.

Ought to be a copper statue out there in the sun, if you ask me.

But I'll tell you something, Yorkie said, leaning and pointing again, and maybe it'll make you feel better and maybe it won't, but I believe it with my whole goddamn heart. I tell you, Chief, people like that? Whoever it was? Whoever was out there defiling her grave? Whoever pulled that shit? They're gonna get theirs.

You said it.

That's how this business works.

Hear, hear, Dean said, throwing back the last of the coffee and preparing to head for the door.

Just you wait and see, Yorkie said, standing. Things like this? They have a way of coming back around.

Dean let himself back out into the sun and it felt good to get a lungful of clean air. Yorkie stepped out from the door and gave Dean a halfhearted wave as he opened the door to his cruiser. He stood there for a moment and watched the sow in the pen grinding her hindquarters on the wooden slats. She squealed as she worked against the hard board and then turned and got to work on the other side.

Chapter 16

They stopped at the Jiff-E station on the main strip and Carp manned the gas while Wallace carried the cooler over to the ice machine off to the side of the building. It was a small structure, no bigger than an armoire, with a metal chute that hung out like a tongue. Wallace opened the cooler and popped a couple of quarters into the machine's slot. There was a button that said DISPENSE ICE and when he pressed it an avalanche of it came pouring out. He was watching the cooler fill when he heard someone talking over the noise.

Getting you some night fishing in?

He looked up. It was a man in a city work shirt, dried mud caked on his chest. In his hand was a can of Milwaukee's Best.

You bet, Wallace said back.

Be a good night for it, the man said. Gonna get kind of cold, if the news is to be believed.

That's just fine, Wallace said. The ice had stopped, so he bent down and closed the cooler. You have you a good one, he said.

Yeah, the man said, ambling closer, if I didn't have the old lady back home, I'd probably load up and join ya.

I hear ya.

Wallace picked up the cooler and started to walk by the man, who was busy with a swig of beer. Up close he looked familiar, like somebody Wallace had split a few pitchers with once upon a time. He thought maybe his name was Murphy or Morris.

Life's a bitch, the man said. 'Specially if you marry one.

Murphy, Wallace thought. Definitely Shawn Murphy. That'd been one of the things he liked to say early in the evening and it'd get a big laugh before he drove it into the ground. He was a real piece of work when he wanted to be and Wallace wanted to get out of there.

See ya later, he said and returned to the car.

Carp was seated behind the wheel, the engine running already. Wallace slipped the cooler into the backseat, right next to the hacksaw, and got inside himself. They were rolling forward when there was a tap on the window. Outside was Murphy with a big, dumb grin across his face. Carp looked at Wallace, who shook his head.

The window rolled down and Murphy, arm thrown across the roof of the car, said, You ain't got you no rods in this car.

Excuse me? Carp said, his voice already on edge.

You and your buddy here, you goin' fishin' aren't ya?

That's right, Wallace said. Got our equipment out at the lake.

Right on, Murphy said and brought the can back up to his mouth. That's a good set-up right there. My brother-in-law keeps an RV parked out by Airline. We go out there every Saturday or so until we can't fish anymore and pass out in the back.

Wallace studied Carp's face. Already his patience was used up. His hand was hovering above the console. Inside was his pistol.

We need to go, Carp said to Murphy.

Which lake y'all headed to? he said. Maybe I'll head out that way later if I can talk my way past the old lady.

We're leaving, Carp said.

What's that? Murphy said.

Wampler, Wallace said. We'll be out bass hunting at Wampler.

Murphy took another drink of his beer and nodded. That's the place to do it. You guys kick some ass out there. Maybe I'll swing by later. Bring some provisions, he said and held up his can before crushing it and tossing it toward the road.

You bet, Wallace said.

Carp drove off before Murphy could walk away. They were back on the road in a matter of seconds, Carp maneuvering into a heavy line of traffic without so much as tapping the brake.

Sorry 'bout that, Wallace said.

Old friends of yours?

Nah, Wallace said. Well, kind of, but I don't think he recognized me.

I would've enjoyed killing him.

Yeah, I don't doubt that. Imagine a lot of people share that opinion.

They drove past the Wal-Mart and the hospital and to the edge of town. The sun was settling in and there was just enough light for them to prepare their weapons. In the trunk was the Remington pump-action Carp had lifted at the storage space, along with a Bobtail he'd wrapped with tape. Wallace loaded his Desert Eagle and considered, for a moment, doing the same with the Bushmaster. Unless Yorkie Goodman was some sort of Rambo, prepper-type, and there was no evidence to the fact, he wasn't going to call for an all-out assault. But Wallace didn't like the way Carp was looking at him, the way he talked to him, so he shoved a magazine into the Bushmaster and went ahead and clicked the safety off for good measure.

When they were finished, Carp drove them to the parking lot of the hospital and they waited in a space. They didn't talk or listen to the radio. They sat and watched the digital numbers on the car's clock turn and melt into one another.

Chapter 17

Yorkie said goodbye to his son and hung up the phone. I'm huntin' tonight, he'd told Michael. Chief Dean was round here today sayin' there might be some methheads raiding my ammonia. Well, his boy had said, be careful. Careful? he said. I ain't the one needs to be careful.

Before he went outside with his double-barrel, he stopped by the fridge and looked at the six-pack cooling on the shelf. One of those Busch Lights sounded pretty good, but he knew he needed to keep his head straight if he was gonna put a scare into those sons of bitches. Instead, he grabbed a slice of bologna and some bread and took that out with him onto the stoop in front of his house.

There was a pair of lawn chairs out there from when he and Janice had used to sit together at night. She'd have herself a gin and tonic – two of them were more than enough to knock her out – and he'd bring a whole six-pack out with him and they'd sit there, in silence for the most part, and just listen to all the sounds. In the spring it was the birds singing in the trees, the cicadas in the summer, and in the fall the geese escaping overhead. Every now and then Janice would give one of her little sighs and say, Well, Yorkie, this is most certainly nice.

It sure is, he'd say back.

All of the lights were off in and outside of Yorkie's

house. He was enveloped in complete darkness as he rested in his chair, the shotgun lying across his lap. He trained his ear the way his daddy had taught him when they'd gone squirrel hunting all those years ago. Listen for the leaves, he thought. Just a crinkle or three.

Sitting out there lulled Yorkie into a state of relaxation. It got so that he could barely keep his eyes open after awhile. Pretty soon he closed them and had a dream that lasted only a split-second but seemed to go on forever. In it he was sitting in the stands with Janice at a track meet and watching Slip win race after race after race. He was the fastest guy out there by a long shot and, whenever he came around the turn, Yorkie and everyone else would stand and cheer and scream their heads off as the school band started to play the fight song to accompany Slip bursting through the finish line. But Slip wouldn't stop. Just as soon as he'd win, he'd speed up again and the race would start all over. He must've won a dozen races by the time Yorkie woke with a start.

Yorkie stretched and rubbed his eyes. Goddamn, he thought, Yorkie, you're getting old.

Deciding it was time to get to bed, Yorkie got up from the chair and went for the door. He reached for the handle to the screen door and, just when he did, he heard the telltale sound of a rustle in the leaves. It wasn't a crinkle though, the sound of a squirrel scurrying through, but a crunch.

Like boots.

Hello? he yelled. Who's that?

The crunch stopped.

Listen, he yelled. If that's a bunch of druggies come to raid my shit, you got another thing coming. I got a double-barrel worth of shot here with your name on it.

Yorkie saw the flash come through the trees and felt, in a great hot instant, the .45 caliber bullet rip through his pelvis. He dropped the shotgun and fell to the ground and wailed and rolled and bit through the tip of his tongue.

A pair of figures materialized out of the woods. They were dressed in black and in his agony Yorkie could only make out their outlines. He heard one of them say, Inside? There was no answer, but soon he was dragged by his arms into the house. The lights came on in a few seconds and the men stood over him, clad in black sweatshirts and jeans, black masks hiding their faces.

Yorkie Goodman, one of them said, we're here to settle an account.

He stared up at the ceiling and tried to concentrate on a single spot. The pain was blinding and it felt like the lower half of his body was disintegrating. Fuck you, he said. I don't owe anybody shit.

The man who'd spoken to him squatted down and removed his mask. His face was pale, like that of a corpse's. Yorkie looked into his eyes and felt like he was staring into a dark mirror. I'm afraid you're mistaken, the man said.

The other man disappeared for a second and when he returned he was carrying a hacksaw and a cooler. He set them next to Yorkie and pointed at them. I want to make this real clear, he said. I want you to know exactly what's going to happen here.

Fuck you, Yorkie spit again, blood starting to bubble out from between his lips.

Here in a few minutes, we're gonna take this hacksaw and we're gonna cut off your fucking head.

You should know, the maskless man said, that you're going to be alive throughout. Until we sever your spinal column you will be alert and you will be awake.

Yorkie tried to sit up, but as he did, the wound in his hip screamed and he fell back and his head hit the floor. He realized that what the men were telling him was true. He knew in a short passage of time he was going to be dead. Getting there was going to be the worst pain he'd ever felt, so he bashed the back of his head on the floor and tried to cave it in. He wanted to beat them to the punch and end it himself. But the maskless man looked down at him and smiled.

Now, now, he said. Don't spoil the fun.

The maskless man rolled Yorkie over onto his stomach and his partner joined him. He felt his hands and ankles being tied with a length of rope. He thought about what was coming and he sobbed and closed his eyes.

Open your eyes, a voice said.

No, Yorkie said and felt the teeth of the saw on his neck. Fuck you. If I'm gonna die, I'm gonna die on my own goddamn terms.

No, the voice said. This isn't about you. You've made your choices. I want you to know who's doing this. I want you to see his face.

Something made Yorkie open his eyes and when he did he was looking at a photograph of a fat man. Though he couldn't remember the name off-hand, he knew him from somewhere. Wait, he said. Who is that?

His name is Boss Valentine, the maskless man said as he held the photograph in front of Yorkie's face.

Wait, Yorkie said again. I know him. Sure as shit. That's Tubby Valentine.

The maskless man looked past Yorkie to his partner. For the first time he seemed confused. You're mistaken, he said. His name is Boss Valentine.

That's Tubby, Yorkie said, remembering a time, years before, where he'd stood on the playground and backed down a smaller, younger, chubbier boy.

Hey, the man holding Yorkie down said, you want to handle this?

With an air of disdain, the maskless man looked at his partner again. Certainly, he said.

The maskless man and his partner traded places. The partner took control of the picture and made sure Yorkie was staring at it. Yorkie, nearly unconscious, was struggling to remember what the fight had been about. Maybe it was a look the boy had given him. Maybe it was the appearance of the boy. He wasn't sure. All he could remember was that he'd knocked Tubby to the ground and straddled him and slapped the shit out of him until his lip was busted and he'd vomited all over himself. He wished he could remember exactly what had happened until he realized it was beyond him, that it was buried under all those years, and that maybe it had been one of those things, something boys needed to get out of their systems, something beyond explanation.

The hacksaw bit into his neck and what the maskless man had said to him was true. He felt everything – the skin giving way, the sawing of the blade, the muscle and fat separating like a great, fleshy seal – until the hacksaw broke through his vertebrae. Look, the partner said one last time and thrust the photograph closer. Yorkie did as he was told and looked, looked deep into the face of the man he could barely remember, the boy he'd bested and forgotten.

Chapter 18

The head slumped forward and then rolled gingerly onto its side. From where Wallace was crouched, it seemed like it was staring into the kitchen. Out of instinct he reached down and grasped it by the hair and lifted it – heavier than he'd thought – and brought the eyes around so he could get a good look.

Put that down, Carp said.

Wallace looked at Carp, his hands and face and the front of his sweatshirt slick with Yorkie's blood. He still had a hold of the hacksaw, angled like a mad claw.

Just putting it away, Wallace said.

You don't get to touch it, Carp said. You don't get the honor.

Something about Carp's tone struck him wrong. It had grown sinister.

Wallace swallowed the lump of fear in his throat and reached for the gun in the waistband of his jeans. Honor? he said, cocking the hammer. What the fuck're you talking about, Carp?

In one fluid motion Carp rose from his position and bent his head so that he was staring at Wallace like an angry bull. The hacksaw fell from his hand and clanked to the bloody floor. Wallace, he said, taking a step toward him, give me the head.

Hold your horses, Wallace said and took a step

back. Just gonna put it on ice.

That's his trophy, Carp said. That's his trophy and I want it to be perfect.

Wallace's back was almost against the rear wall of Yorkie's living room. He watched Carp reach for his gun and said, Hold the fuck on, Carp. Don't reach for that goddamn gun.

It was in your file, Carp said. You knew the rules. You knew the score, Wallace. You were told, expressly, what you weren't to do.

With his free hand Wallace leveled his gun at Carp. The head hung at his side and for a moment he felt it start to slip but he cinched his grip and got a handful of the old man's slick hair. You come near me, he said, and I swear to God, Carp, I'll blow your crazy fucking head off.

Without so much as a pause Carp took another step. In that step he moved to pull out his weapon and Wallace squeezed the trigger. The shot hit Carp square in the mouth and spun him like a top, sending him into a crazed twirl that deposited him on the floor next to Yorkie's bleeding body. He hit with a sick thud and soon his blood and Yorkie's mixed in an ever-growing ocean.

Still high on adrenaline, Wallace carried the head over to the cooler and shoved it down into the ice. He ran out of the house and through the woods and the cemetery, aware of every step and the sloshing and crunching of the head in the cooler. As he made his way to the car – parked on a dirt road on the other side of Fairview – he couldn't help but feel something chasing him. His ears fooled him into thinking he could hear footfalls, panting breath, and his nerves told him it was Carp. But when he looked back his eyes told another story. There was no one and nothing at his heels, just dark night and the ground he'd already tread.

Chapter 19

Chief Dean was considering the deputy's question from earlier in the day – how was he going to keep on pulling these double-shifts? – when a black car sped by him on the country road. His first thought was to flip on the reds and blues and pull it over. But quickly that thought changed to an even more urgent question of his own.

Had he, in the headlights of his car, just seen the face of Bill Wallace?

Dean punched his brakes and came to a skidding stop. He had a grip on the wheel with both hands. They were shaking, both of them, so he let go and then rubbed his eyes with the balls of his fists. When he looked again, the empty road was lit up and strange shadows were moving on the edges of his headlights.

Hell no, he thought. There's no way you just saw Bill Wallace. Son of a bitch is probably dead. And if it happens he's alive, he ain't dumb enough to step foot in this state, let alone this town, again.

With that, he pressed the gas again and the car rolled forward. In his mind he replayed the moment again and again and every time he did he couldn't help but see Bill Wallace's face. He told himself it was the mind seeing what the mind wanted to see. It was something he was familiar with, what with being in law enforcement. Witnesses misidentified suspects all the time. People had a habit of making mistakes.

On down the road Dean pulled the cruiser into Yorkie Goodman's field again and cut the lights. He rolled down the window and turned the radio on just above a whisper. There was a call-in show playing and the host was talking to callers about their finances. The first one Dean heard asked the host whether his retirement was safe in the stock market.

There's no such thing as safe, the host said. But you have to have trust at some point. You have to put your faith in people every now and then.

Dean, who was pouring himself a cup of coffee out of his thermos, laughed. You try and trust those fuckers, he said, and you're likely to end up bleeding in a gutter somewhere.

The next few callers asked questions about investments and when it was the host's turn to speak Dean just drank his coffee and shook his head. He didn't know why he listened to shit that pissed him off, but it was something he couldn't cure himself of doing.

All right, the host said after a call, let's welcome to the air Bill from Pittsburgh.

Again, Dean thought of the face in the black car. When he remembered it, all he could see was Bill Wallace. He picked up the receiver to his radio and got ahold of dispatch. Dispatch, he said when they picked up, this is Chief Dean.

Howdy Chief, came the voice over the radio. It was Doug Harper, a patrolman Dean couldn't trust for shit. He'd been a detective the better part of six months before evidence started disappearing. But his uncle was on the city council and so he got to keep his cruiser and badge. What can I do you for? he said.

Evening, Harper, Dean said. Do me a favor and get out the Bill Wallace folder for me. Set it on my desk so I can get a look at it tomorrow.

Done and done, Harper said. You working some overtime?

You got it, he said. Somebody's got to clean the shitter.

When he put the receiver back, he looked up and tried to get his eyes to focus on the dark. He didn't figure he was going to have any luck catching the juvenile delinquents who'd desecrated his mama's grave. It was a sad truth he'd been keenly aware of from the beginning. Chances were it was a one-time fling and wasn't going to be a habit. It was getting colder, anyhow, and the odds of just sitting out in the field and waiting night after night paying off were astronomical. Still though, he sat and watched and hoped maybe he was wrong.

It was hard settling his eyes though. Off to the side of Fairview, through the limbs in the bare trees, there was a light on at Yorkie Goodman's house. It glowed like an eye in the night and that glow was just enough to keep Dean from being able to see through the dark.

The clock on the radio told him it was a quarter 'til midnight. Too late for an old man to be up, he said to himself. Course, you're up.

Shut your mouth, he said aloud.

For some reason he couldn't stop looking at the light on at Yorkie's. Nothing about it seemed particularly suspicious or that out of the ordinary, but that voice of his was starting to weigh in.

Dean, it said, you know as well as I do that ain't right.

That so? he said to the voice.

Sure as shit. And you're thinking 'bout it now and you know there's something strange 'bout that light. Wasn't there some suspicious people by there the night before? Say they went back, Dean. Say they decided to knock on the door.

I hear what you're saying, he said, but I ain't convinced.

Shouldn't be that bad a thing to go and knock on the door yourself. Just to check in.

I don't aim to do any such thing, Dean said.

And why not?

Cause you might be right, he said.

The radio show went to a commercial for a local car lot. The voiceover was loud and, when it got done talking, a trumpet played like a big parade was getting ready to start. Come and see us, the voice-over said.

All right then, Dean said.

As he got out of the cruiser, he was suddenly aware of how quiet the world was at that time of night. Out in the country there was nothing but the occasional howl of a coyote or a plane cruising over. Other than that, it was just sky and stars and the sound of your own breath. Dean thought again of Wallace, of how much he didn't want to walk on over to Yorkie's, and then started walking.

By the time he got to Yorkie's front door, Dean was a bit winded. Lack of sleep was starting to catch up to him and so was age. He wasn't made for burning the midnight oil anymore. Hell, he wasn't much made for burning the morning or afternoon oil for that matter. He was getting heavy, slow, his knee growing worse by the day. He stood on the steps he'd climbed that morning and paused before he knocked.

You don't want to, the voice said, but you need to.

Let me make up my own damn mind about what I want to do, he thought and then knocked on the door.

He listened for the sound of Yorkie shuffling through the house. For any sound.

Hey, he called. Hey, Yorkie, you all right in there?

A sense of dread washed over him then and he surveyed the door for any kind of damage. It was clean, but when he looked out into the yard he could see a shotgun laying in the tall grass.

Yorkie, he yelled and unholstered his gun, I'm coming in.

With a well-placed kick at the spot next to the knob, Dean knocked the door open and splintered the frame. The first thing he saw was everything. All the blood. The pair of bodies. The hacksaw. The empty space where Yorkie Goodman's head had once been.

Jesus God, Dean cried out of reflex. Oh, Jesus, God in heaven.

He neared the massacre and looked at Yorkie again. He stared at where his head should have been and looked from his neck to the blood-covered floor. He did this a half-dozen times and still couldn't understand what he was looking at. Then he looked at the body next to Yorkie's. It was face down and dressed all in black. When he turned it over, he could see that the man's jaw had been destroyed. Bone and teeth lay scattered everywhere like bits of shell on a beach.

Dean pulled his radio. I need backup to Yorkie Goodman's farm, he said. Get out here in a hurry. Route 2 right next to Fairview cemetery. Hurry.

He couldn't stand there for too long. It was too grisly of a scene and his stomach was already knotting and flipping. He walked carefully back to the front door and relived himself in the weeds off to the side of the steps. He retched until he couldn't retch anymore and crouched there wiping his mouth and eyes with the handkerchief he kept in his back pocket. Then he sat in the open front door trying to learn how to breathe again. He was thinking about how he wasn't going to listen to that goddamn voice anymore, how he needed to find himself a new line of work. He was so occupied that he didn't hear one of the bodies lifting itself off the floor.

Chapter 20

For reasons that escaped him, Carp swept up what he could of his teeth and jaw off the floor and shoved them into his pocket. He lifted himself up and turned and saw the policeman doubled-over near the doorway. He walked carefully, quietly, toward him. A step or so away he balled up his fist and slammed it into the policeman's left temple. The policeman rocked to his right and hit the doorway and slumped down. Carp watched to make sure he was still breathing. The last thing he needed was a dead officer on his hands.

Outside he slunk into Yorkie Goodman's truck and found the keys still in the ignition. He turned it on and punched the gas, sending a spray of dirt and gravel into the side of the house. When he got onto the road, and had left the scene behind him, he turned the rearview mirror and saw that the lower half of his face was a disfigured, gory mess. The right side of his jaw looked like it'd been hacked at by a discount butcher. Blood leaked down onto his already saturated sweatshirt.

He pulled into the parking lot of the hospital, where he and Wallace had waited earlier. He pulled out his cell and texted Boss.

Shot cant talk need med help @ hosp.

Seconds later a message appeared: 5 minutes.

Four minutes later Carp watched the automatic

door open and an older man with stark-white hair hurried out. He was wearing blue ER scrubs and carrying a plastic bag. Carp blinked his lights twice and the older man made a beeline for him and opened up the passenger seat.

Goddamn, the man said when he got his first look at Carp. Oh, fuck. You need to go inside. Holy shit.

Carp shook his head and mumbled with great pain, Do it here.

I don't think I can, the man said. Listen, I know you don't want the attention, but you're in trouble. Holy shit, I mean, real trouble.

Carp pointed at his jaw and said again, Do it here.

I don't think you understand. There's not a lot I can do here.

As soon as he had said it, Carp grabbed the man and pulled him in close, close enough so that their noses touched and blood from his wound landed on the man's face as Carp said, Fucking. Do it. Here.

With that the man began to work. He pulled out a roll of gauze, an antiseptic and some stitching materials. He did his best to disinfect the wound, but had to stop to lean out the door and vomit. He apologized and returned to his job, dabbing the exposed tissue and tying off the bleeding wherever he could.

Carp sat silently as the man worked. He pictured the pain as a marble he could pick up between his fingers and roll around in his palm. When it spiked or became too much, he simply pitched the marble away until it rolled back to him. From time to time police cars roared by with their lights and sirens howling through the night.

An hour later the man said he'd done all he could. Carp looked at himself and the giant blood-soaked bandage covering a chunk of his face.

It's going to get infected, the man said. I can't help that. And if you don't get immediate help, soon, you're going to lose your jaw. Maybe more.

That's fine, Carp said. You're done here.

The man wasted no time in gathering his supplies and exiting the truck. He walked back into the hospital, scratching his head as he went.

Carp picked up his phone and dialed Boss' number.

You good? Boss said when he picked up.

I'm fine, Carp mumbled. Wallace double-crossed me.

That's what we figured, right? We'll take care of him in good order. Bring the head back and we'll get things lined up.

Carp grimaced with a sudden jolt of pain. He's got the head.

What the fuck're you talking about? Boss said. What do you mean he's got the head?

He shot me. Right in the face. I'll get it back.

Boss went silent. Then Carp heard a sound like he'd punched a wall. I'll call in ten. We've got tracking on the car. We'll get you a location on him and we'll try other measures if necessary.

You got it, Carp said and hit the button to end his call.

He drove back to the hotel and loaded up his bags. Everywhere he looked there were signs of him and

Wallace. Hair. Luggage. Toiletries. He looked in the mirror at himself and thought he looked near death.

As he was throwing his bags into the bed of Yorkie's truck, Carp noticed a pair of gasoline cans. He grabbed one in each hand and carried them back into the room. He splashed the floor and walls and beds with gas and tossed the cans and what was left of the gas into the bathroom. There was a pack of complimentary matches on the table by the door. He grabbed them on his way out and set the pack on fire and threw it into the room. The shockwave of the ignition hit his body as he made for the truck. The room went up in an instant, the flames growing and climbing and the wallpaper rolling in the heat.

Carp got into the truck and pulled out of the lot just as everyone started gathering outside their rooms to watch. He looked at his cell and saw a text from Boss. It read SOUTH. He turned around in the middle of stunted traffic – most of the drivers slowing down to get an eyeful of the growing blaze – and piloted the truck in that direction. As he did, he felt something jostle in his pocket. He reached in and found a bloody mess of teeth and bone in his hand. Rolling down the window, he reached out and let the night air blow it all away.

Chapter 21

The cabin sat on the outskirts of Little Nashville, a tourist community made up of small souvenir and trinket shops and surrounded by hills used for skiing in the heart of winter. It was still pitch black when Wallace pulled into the city limits and stopped at a Citgo station. His clothes were stiff with dried sweat. His heart still thumping hard. He walked into the gas station and got a couple of six-packs out of the cooler and set them on the counter. A boy of maybe seventeen was working the overnight shift and when he saw the beer he shook his head and said, Past midnight, can't sell.

Huh, Wallace said and fished a hundred out of his pocket, sounds like a pretty tough rule.

The boy took the hundred and stuffed it into his jeans. You need gas?

Just a splash of it, Wallace said. And a bag of ice.

Outside he opened up the freezer by the door and got a ten-pound bag. He dropped it on the ground a few times until the cubes were broken loose and then carried it over to the black Ford. The cooler was sitting in the backseat and he took it out and opened the top. There was the head, still half-buried, the hair sticking up like a mess of antennae.

He reached in and held the head in place while he dumped out the old ice. The feeling of it made him a touch sick and he was quick to pour in the new bag. A thought had occurred to him during the drive and he got in the trunk and found the electrical tape he and Carp had used to tape the grips of their guns. He rolled a strip around the top of the cooler to keep any of the cold from getting out and put the cooler back on the seat.

Everything told him to get back into the car and hurry. Ever since he shot Carp he'd been possessed of a fear that quickened his movements and kept his adrenaline driving, but standing there at the pump he felt like he had slipped a noose of sorts. He felt like it was time to take a deep breath and revel in the moment. Carp was dead. Boss was in North Carolina, probably having a shit fit, but nothing was going to happen to him as long as he had the head. And besides, if his luck held out, Carol was waiting for him just a few miles away.

The street running next to the gas station was mostly empty except for some work trucks rolling by. A police cruiser was among them and Wallace watched it for a second before deciding it was just a drowsy officer out making the rounds. He finished gassing up the Ford and was off again.

As he reached the main strip of the town, he allowed himself, for the first time, to turn on the radio. First it was local news and he listened to see if Yorkie Goodman had made the cut. He hadn't and after it ended he flipped the channel and came across an Eagles' song. Hey, he said to the cooler, you an Eagles' fan by any chance?

The cooler didn't respond.

The strip was black except for a few streetlamps

throwing halos onto the sidewalks. He hadn't seen it so desolate since Carol and he had snuck down, drunk as a pair of skunks, back in the late Nineties. Little Nashville had been their stomping ground back then, particularly when her family stayed at the cabin for the holidays. They'd get nice and soused and then go joy riding. The local police looked the other way when it came to that sort of thing because they wanted to be tourist-friendly, so most stops ended in a lecture and a polite inquiry whether the driver knew his way home.

But Wallace had run into a little trouble when he and Carol broke into one of the cheesy jewelry stores. They'd spent the day drinking on the strip and going from shop to shop, looking at all the airbrushed T-shirts and faux-turquoise knick-knacks. Carol had mentioned she liked a pair of feather earrings. She'd touched Wallace's shoulder and pointed at them, saying, They look like peacocks, don't they?

Sure, Wallace said. Just like a peacock. Reckon they picked 'em fresh?

Carol had slugged him in the arm and when Wallace asked if she wanted a pair she'd told him no, they weren't the kind of thing she'd wear anyway and it'd just be a waste of his money.

But that night, after everyone had gone to bed, the two of them had been laying under the covers and Carol turned to him and said, I should've bought those damn earrings.

The peacock ones?

Yeah, she said. I really liked those. Call me crazy, but I thought they were pretty.

Wallace, full of whiskey and youth, threw off the sheets and said, Get your shoes on, honey.

The store with the earrings was called Beautiful Memories and Wallace had broken the glass in the front door and reached in and unlocked it. It was too dark, so Carol turned on the light. They were just standing over those earrings, the peacock ones, when an off-duty cop told them to freeze.

They were both hauled into the Brown County jail and booked, but Carol's dad – a county judge – came in and washed her name clean. The judge had never been fond of Wallace though and left him in for the night. The next morning he had to call a buddy of his in Bloomington to come and pony up bail.

Wallace thought about how the judge died a couple of years after that. The judge sitting in the living room of his house, all his family and friends gathered to watch him suffer away, cancer filthy through his stomach and colon. Wallace remembered sitting in the kitchen, away from everybody, sipping Red Label and counting down the minutes.

Past the strip, the road turned curvy and Wallace navigated the stretch and kept an eye on the signs. Most of the cabins were rentals and labeled with some sort of happy-go-lucky nickname. Maple Rest. Hilltop View. Mountain Delight. But Carol's cabin stuck out from the rest. Instead of a smiling honeybee sign or a strawberry or healthy-looking pine, there was just a rustic wooden sign with the words JUDGE'S QUARTERS. Wallace saw it and turned the Ford down the dirt road.

The cabin was a half mile down, a gray two-story

home with a wraparound porch that looked out over a gulch and a winding creek. It was secluded and beautiful, one of Wallace's favorite places in all the world. Just looking at it made him smile, and it only helped when he saw Carol's red pickup parked in the driveway.

He got out of the car and brought the beer and the cooler. When he got to the front door, he went to knock but a voice yelled at him that it was open. He walked in and all the lights were off save for the one in the kitchen. The air smelled musty, like the windows hadn't been opened in years. He navigated the darkness to the kitchen door. Carol was sitting at the butcher-block table in the kitchen, smoking a cigarette and drinking a glass of vodka and ice.

Hey there, Wallace said and put the beer and cooler down. Ain't you a sight for sore eyes.

Carol took a final drag of her cigarette and stubbed it out in a glass ashtray. She took a deep breath and Wallace watched her body deflate and then inflate in one motion. Cut the bullshit, she said. What am I doing here?

Wallace nodded to let her know that he knew it was a legitimate question and got to work putting the beer in the fridge. In the fridge he saw some lunchmeat, fruit, eggs, bacon, sausage. Enough for a week, at least. He loaded in the beer and got a can off one of the six-packs and had a drink. It tasted good, so he had one more. What? he said after. No 'it's good to see you?' No 'goddamn Bill, you're looking good?'

She looked away from him and out a black window looking toward the back of the house. She rapped her knuckles on the butcher block and then said, I took a chance coming here, Bill. Either you start telling me what's going on or I leave. And I call the police before I go.

Sitting the can of beer on the butcher-block, Wallace leaned across and touched Carol's chin with his fingers. She flinched away and gave him a glare. Well, he said, I can't help but be happy to see you. Even if you're not too pleased to see me, I have to say that I've been thinking about this a long time.

Carol's face changed and for a second she seemed to warm. Then her eyes shifted and narrowed. Bill, she said. What's in the cooler?

Wallace nudged the cooler away with his boot. Nothing, he said. Nothing we need to talk about right now, anyway. If you want to talk, let's talk. Ask me anything you want to ask me. I'll do my best.

All right, she said. Where've you been for fourteen years?

Carolina, he said. After the whole thing with Wilcox, I had to leave.

That's fine, she said, her eyes hardened, but why didn't you take me?

You want the truth? he said. Or do you want me to bullshit you?

Of course I want you to bullshit me. That's what I want, Bill. A big load of bullshit.

Well, he said, I could do that. I could sit here and feed you a line of bullshit. I could tell you what I think you want to hear or I can tell you what happened. I'm sure you've got your version of how things worked out and I got mine. I can tell you mine or I can just sit here and lie 'til morning and we won't get anywhere.

The truth, she said. Tell me the truth.

I'll tell you, he said, but you got to promise you're not gonna get up and walk away. You and I both know you got a temper on ya. You got to remember it's been a long time since I left. We're talking about a lot of time for a lot of things to happen.

What? she said. You get hitched?

Yeah, he said and drummed his fingers on the table. I did.

Carol slapped Wallace hard across the face. What's her name?

Does it matter?

I think it does, she said, her face getting red. If my fucking husband gets married again, I think I have a right to know her goddamn name.

I don't know why you need to know.

I do. And that's my business.

Cindy, he said. Her name's Cindy.

All right, she said. You got a kid?

Got two of 'em.

Two kids? Fuck you.

Now don't say that.

I wait fourteen years for your worthless ass to come back around and you're out starting a families and doing God knows what.

It isn't like that, he said. It is, but it isn't. Truth is, I stayed away to try and keep you safe. You know the kind of people I work with.

I know all too well, Carol said.

Well, they ain't the kind of people who let someone take off, he said and then paused like he'd just realized something. I mean, Carol, they ain't the kind who wave goodbye and let you ride on out into the sunset.

Carol fished her pack of cigarettes out of her pocket and lit another one. She took a drag and let the smoke tumble from her lips. If that's true, she said, then what're you doing here?

You know what I was thinking about? he said, changing the subject.

What's that?

On the way in tonight, I was thinking about that time you and me broke into that shop on the strip. The jewelry store with the peacock feather earrings.

I loved those things, she said. But that was a hell of a mess you got me into.

The judge wasn't too happy, was he? he said.

Let's not talk about him, she said and then pointed at the cooler. So, she said, what's in there?

Let's not talk about that either, he said.

All right, she said, then tell me how the hell you're so sure the people you work with are gonna let you go this time. Or is this just a pit stop?

No, he said and had a drink. If you're willing, I think I just want to stay here with you. Or go somewhere with you, doesn't matter to me.

The jury's still out, she said.

I figured that, he said, but we at least got the option.

How so?

Because of what's in the cooler, he said.

And what's in the cooler?

You really want to know?

She said, Maybe.

If you want to know I'll tell you.

All right, she said. I want to know.

Wallace bent down and tore off the tape around the cooler. He opened the top of it and tilted it so Carol could see inside.

Is that what I think it is? she said.

Yeah, he said, I reckon it is.

Chapter 22

And what year is it? the doctor asked Dean.

1954, Dean said and popped his neck. Old Eisenhower's in office and there's no way a black's ever gonna get the job.

Funny, the doctor said and scratched his chin. You took a pretty good thump.

I've taken a few in my day, Dean said. I'm good though. Care if I get out of here?

The doctor looked around the room. Outside, in the ER, the nurses and attendants were doing their best to talk quietly about the body at Yorkie Goodman's farm. Dean could hear them though, could hear the words 'massacre' and 'headless.' The doctor said, pretty grisly scene, huh?

You don't know the half of it, Dean said and slid off the examination table. He grabbed his coat and slipped his arms through the sleeves.

Well, the doctor said, good news is you don't have to go by there tonight. Run home, get some rest. I'm sure you'll have a whole mess of trouble waiting on you tomorrow.

I'm sure I will, Dean said and walked to the door.

As he made his way out of the ER he was aware of people staring. He checked with the reception desk whether they needed anything else from him. He met Bockwinkel at the automatic doors. He was holding his hat in his hands and looked as jolted as anybody

Dean had ever laid eyes on.

You all right? he asked.

Sure, Bockwinkel said, though his tone wasn't convincing. I'm just fine, Chief.

You run out to the scene? Dean said.

Bockwinkel stared into the corner of the room. Yeah, he said. Reckon I did.

Yep, Dean said.

The two of them went out the doors to where Bockwinkel's cruiser was parked and Dean was about to maneuver himself inside, when a man in a Butler Bulldogs windbreaker reached out and touched him on the arm. Chief, he said, I'm with the Indy Star.

No comment, Dean said. Nothing for y'all 'til morning.

Just tell me, the man said, is it as bad as what they're saying?

Dean got into the car and said, Sure thing.

What's your condition?

Pretty damn bad.

You get a look at the fella?

No, Dean said, but I'm fixin' to get an eyeful before this whole thing finishes out.

Bockwinkel drove to Dean's house without so much as saying another word. That was fine with Dean because he was focused on how all the lights they passed were surrounded by halos. Anytime he got to focusing on one, his head started to hurt worse than it had before and he'd have to close his eyes until the pain laid off. He'd taken a hell of a thump, he knew that, but he wasn't used to having this kind of lingering effect.

Here we go, Chief, Bockwinkel said as they pulled to his house.

Thanks, Bockwinkel.

You need anything? he said. Coffee? Tylenol?

Probably got everything I need in there, Dean said.

Sure thing, Bockwinkel said. Try and get some shuteye. Gonna be a long day tomorrow.

I know that, Dean said and climbed the steps to his house.

When he got inside, he sat on the couch and tried to keep the room from spinning on him. Even the darkness vibrated and pretty soon he felt like he was going to get sick. He went into the bathroom and, as the feeling took over, he was reminded of how it'd been right there before he'd been attacked and he liked to have jumped out of his shoes for not turning around and looking.

You ain't gonna get any rest, the voice said to him.

No, he said back, don't figure I will.

Could've been killed.

Sure as shit could've.

And whoever done it, the voice said, is still running round.

Sure as shit, he said.

Dean got a comb out and ran it through his hair a few times and then brushed his teeth. He took off his uniform and switched it out with a clean one hanging on the closet door. He got in the Dodge he kept in the driveway and though he hadn't driven it regularly for a few years and the tires were bald as hell, he rode into the station and parked in his reserved space.

The station itself was deserted. Dean figured most everyone was out at the scene or being briefed at the county courthouse. He thought of all that blood and his body shook. Yorkie Goodman was lying there like a piece of meat. Dean had been there just that morning, drinking coffee and shooting the shit.

What was it Yorkie said? the voice asked him.

About what?

About the world?

Yorkie was saying a lot of shit about the world.

No, the voice said, about things coming back around.

That's just what he said, Dean said. Just exactly what he said.

The phone on his desk rang. He picked it up and it was a reporter out of Terre Haute. Word is you walked in on two bodies, he said.

Shitfire, Dean said, looks like one of them walloped me right on the head.

He hung up the phone and sat back in his seat. He couldn't do the math on this one. Yorkie Goodman, some bumfuck farmer, sprawled out and missing a head. Some other sonuvabitch next to him, his jaw shot to hell and bleeding like a stuck pig.

It sounded like an old joke. Something he'd heard in boot camp maybe, or something one of his corny ass uncles used to tell.

A man and his buddy walk in and find the man's wife on the ground, her head rolled over next to her body.

Is she dead? the man asks his buddy.

If she ain't, the buddy says, she's damn near on

her way.

Dean didn't laugh. Didn't seem funny anymore.

The phone rang again. It was a detective with the state police. Chief Dean? he said.

You sound surprised.

I was aiming to get your voicemail.

Well, you got me.

All right, the detective said. You gonna be there for a while?

Figure I'll be here all day. Come on by and see me.

You got it, the detective said.

Dean hung up the phone. His head was screaming like there was a ten-piece band tuning up between his temples. He massaged them with his fingers and closed his eyes. When he opened them he was looking at his desk. There was a folder sitting on his calendar marked WALLACE. He remembered the black car that'd raced by him, the face in the headlights. He picked up the folder and began to leaf through it.

Chapter 23

Sleep wouldn't come easy for Wallace. Just as he got situated and closed his eyes and managed to get his heartbeat under control, he'd think of the sound the saw made cutting into Yorkie Goodman's neck and he'd snap up and have to start all over again. If it wasn't that, it was listening to the sounds the woods made outside. Every snap and pop and hoot sounded like Carp sneaking in for the kill.

He had to remind himself that Carp was as dead as dead could be.

He threw back the sheet and stood up from the bed. Carol, true to form, didn't stir a bit. She was out, had been since they'd made up for old times in a frenzy of violent and frantic love. The late-evening moon crept in through the window and painted her a shade of soft silver.

Wallace walked downstairs and got a beer out of the fridge. He took a drink and then another. He grabbed his coat by the door and pulled out his cellphone. When he got to the porch, he hit a button and saw thirty-four missed calls from Cindy. Twenty-eight voicemails. Twenty messages. He sat on the railing of the porch and considered his options.

Part of him knew he should call her and at least give her a heads up. The guilt of not having done the same for Carol all those years ago had never let go. Got him in this mess, that was for sure. But the conversation would be an ugly one. There were children to consider. He'd have to hear the heartbreak in her voice. The anger. The hurt.

He hit the button to make the call. It was late, and the ringing would wake up the whole family, but he needed to get it done. It was the right thing to do and he knew it.

The phone rang six times and the voicemail picked up. It was his own voice asking him to leave a message.

He hit the button to cancel the call and called again.

Six more times. And six more times his voice prompted him to leave a message.

He stood up and walked out into the driveway. The light bounced off of the car and Carol's pickup. He called again and got voicemail.

Something didn't feel right.

It reminded him of a job he'd pulled three years ago. He and a thug named Thursday had driven a stolen car down to Tampa and switched it out for another. Sewed into the lining of the trunk had been a Glock used to kill a patrolman and his brother who'd been competing with Boss' supply line. On the second day of the trip Wallace tried to call Cindy from a gas station outside of Charleston, but didn't have any luck. All day he called and could never get through. Later he found out his boy had nearly died from eating bad shrimp at lunch and Cindy had spent all day praying at his bedside at the hospital.

Wallace remembered and as he did something dark took over.

He put the phone away and tried not to think of the possibilities. There was a long list of awful things. He spit into the gravel and paced.

Then, a sound in the woods. He stopped and felt instantly cold. His skin grew clammy. He tried to make his body move but it wouldn't cooperate. Another sound. He finally turned and faced it. Something scampered off into the trees.

The trunk.

He thought of the job with Thursday and the Glock. He opened the Ford's trunk and pressed into the liner and swept his hand across. There were the usual ridges and bumps. But then, something larger. He went and got a knife out of the kitchen. Stopping to look at the red and white cooler on the floor, he carried the knife outside and sawed a small hole into the liner.

The tracking device was no bigger than a cell phone. Plain black. Three ridges toward the top. He dropped it into the gravel and stomped it to pieces with his boot.

He did the math in his head. Eleven hours. Ten if they really hustled.

There was just enough time to get packed and eat a good breakfast. Maybe a little more than that. Boss needed to mobilize. Bring in something or somebody serious.

He looked out into the woods and caught a hint of the sun rising. The night was glowing and humming, the daytime animals coming alive.

Chapter 24

Boss took the travel mug from Abel and started the car. Last chance, he said. You got any music you want to bring? You got anything you're forgetting?

Nah, Abel said. I'm fine.

You don't listen to music anymore?

I got podcasts.

Podcasts? Boss said. What the hell are you talking about? Podcasts?

Abel said, You know, like radio shows on the Internet.

What a load of shit. Boss put the car into gear and reached out the window to give Simmons, behind the wheel of the U-Haul, the sign to head off. Let me ask you this, Boss said to Abel, is there anything you know besides the goddamn Internet?

Sure, Abel said. I know about a lot of stuff.

You don't know an anthill from your asshole.

Abel shifted in his seat and looked out the window. The sky was lightening and a few of the neighboring houses had lights on. A woman in a jogging suit ran by. So, he said, how's this thing work?

How's it work? Boss said.

Yeah. How's it work?

Well, he said, we're heading to Indiana. You know that much.

And what about the truck?

You know about the truck.

Sure, but I guess I don't know everything.

You don't need to know everything, Boss said. I swear to God, you get Google in peoples' hands and they think they need to know everything. Let me tell you this much, the less you know about the truck the better.

Fine, Abel said, but you don't have to be an asshole about it.

Boss scratched his forehead and then reached down to grab his mug of coffee. He took a sip and it burned his tongue. Shit, he said. Shit, shit, shit. That's gonna be with me a few days. Look here, he said to Abel, I got a reason to be an asshole right now. Last count, I got near a hundred reasons to be a real piece of shit asshole for a couple of hours.

This guy, Abel said, the one we're going to see.

Wallace, Boss said.

Sure, Abel said, Wallace.

What about him?

He gonna be a problem?

Boss put the mug down and looked ahead. The truck was keeping up a good pace and already weaving through traffic. He kept the car a length or two away. Maybe, he said, maybe not. He's pretty reasonable.

He's not Carpenter, Abel said.

Hell no, Boss said, nobody's like Carp. They ain't ever made one like him before and I'll be damned if they ever make another one again. If this was Carp, he said, and it never would be, but if it were, we'd be better off just letting him go.

But this Wallace guy, Abel said.

He's dangerous, but he's reasonable.

So we show up with this truck.

We show up with this truck and we'll see what happens. What you've got to learn, he said, is that you can't always figure how people are gonna react, Abel. You start putting all your eggs in a basket and trying to figure every little detail, you're liable to lose a shitload of eggs.

You always seem to know though.

Goddamn it, he yelled and smacked the steering wheel. The truck had sped up and opened six to seven car lengths of space. Boss pressed the gas and passed a van on the shoulder. Abel, he said, there you go thinking you know something. Next time you think you know shit, do me a favor and keep it to yourself.

Abel pulled out his phone then and checked his e-mail and text folder. He had one text from his mom. It said, Are you sure you want to go? You can always change your mind. He hit the home button on his phone and locked it and put it away in his pocket. I'm trying here, he said.

I know, Boss said. I know you are. Goddamn. Just wish the man would slow down or at least wait until I got a lane.

All right, Abel said, so, your best guess – what's Wallace gonna do?

My best guess?

Yeah.

He's made of hard stuff, Boss said, but he ain't made of the hardest stuff. Guy like him, guy like anybody I guess, he gets confronted by that, chances are he's either gonna either shit his pants or light us up.

Light us up?

Fight or flight, Boss said. It's the most primordial instinct we've got left. The reptilian brain, Abel. You either run the hell away or you stay and throw a few punches.

And which one's it gonna be?

Hell if I know, Boss said and took another drink of his coffee. He got on the truck's bumper and put his hand out the window to flip Simmons off. When he was done, he rolled the window back up and shook his head and laughed. Abel, he said, the older I get the surer I am of a few things: one, you better appreciate your pecker while it's still working the way it's supposed to work. Two, there ain't a man walking the face of this here earth who knows shit about shit.

Sounds good, Abel said.

Sounds awful, Boss said. Now, he said, maybe get one of those fucking podcasts loaded up. Or whatever the hell it is you do with them.

What do you want? Abel said. I got all kinds.

Son, Boss said, just do whatever. I'm not gonna ask again.

Chapter 25

Carp didn't believe in visions but it was hard for him to dispute he was having one.

Lying in the woods, flat on his stomach on the earth and dead leaves, he could see the cabin and its contents. Wallace and Carol were in there preparing their breakfast on the stove.

He could feel everything.

Every movement in the forest.

Every step an ant took along his skin.

The throbbing, stabbing pain where his jaw had been obliterated.

He both slept and didn't sleep. Existence had become a waking dream. At one point he imagined himself a snake crawling out of its skin, worming his shoulders through what had once been his body and birthing into the world as an entirely new species. He was aware that all of his natural tendencies, his desires, his wants, his needs, had been replaced by a singular desire to live long enough to see Wallace killed.

The pain was constant. The ball that had held it had been rolled away so much that it wouldn't roll away any longer. It had gathered more pain until its mass had made it a boulder, a compact network of sensory torture. Carp willed himself to unhinge his jaw and swallowed it whole. The ball worked its slow way down his gullet and into his stomach and he felt it pulsing and growing there. Felt it start to fuel him.

He watched Wallace and Carol in the cabin. They were sitting down. Wallace held a mug of coffee in one hand and a fork in the other. He was gesturing with it. Carp could hear what he was saying from two hundred yards away. He was telling her about tomorrow, about the possibilities of life, of hope.

Carp listened and waited.

Chapter 26

The neighbor yelled to Chief Dean as he was knocking on the door. She said, I think she took off for the weekend.

Huh, Dean said. He turned and watched the neighbor walk across the yard and approach the porch. You have any idea where she took off to?

Well, the neighbor said, maybe. She in some kind of trouble?

Nah, Dean said. I don't think so.

Cause she looked like she was in a pretty good hurry.

How so?

She was carrying a bunch of bags and food out to her truck. Hadn't put on a touch of makeup.

That unusual? Dean said.

Yeah, the neighbor said. She was older, sixty maybe, wearing a sweatshirt with pictures of her grandchildren laminated on the front. You didn't hear it from me, she said, but Carol's a little on the vain side.

Secret's safe, Dean said. What did you say about where she was heading?

I asked her and she said something about getting out of town. Maybe going to stay at her daddy's cabin.

Whereabouts is that?

Chief, the neighbor said, you sure she's not in trouble?

If we're being honest here, Dean said, I don't quite know.

Cause I heard on the news, the neighbor said. They were talking about Yorkie Goodman and everything.

Shame isn't it?

More than a shame, she said. It's a tragedy, Chief. Just plain awful.

Couldn't agree with you more.

You don't think she's in trouble, do ya?

Maybe, Dean said, but I need to talk to her. You have any idea where that cabin is?

Brown County, the neighbor said. Can't tell you much more than that. Little Nashville, maybe. Chief?

Yeah?

What do you think happened out there? At Yorkie's place? My sister-in-law thinks it was drugs. Was it drugs?

You can't tell with this kind of stuff, Dean said. Could've been drugs. Could've been something crazier than that.

Lord almighty, the neighbor said. You know what I think?

What's that?

I think the world's done gone insane.

I'd be inclined to agree. Thank ya for the help, he said.

I mean, she said, I just can't figure how something like that happens.

I can't figure how most things happen anymore.

Amen, the neighbor said, moving to walk back to her yard.

Chapter 27

You haven't asked me anything, Carol said.

Wallace knew it was coming. All through breakfast, ever since they'd woken up, he could tell that something was brewing in her, like the water they'd boiled on the stove for their coffee. He had wanted to ask but was afraid of what conversation that might lead to. What kind of anger it would provoke.

We've got all the time in the world, he said and laid his fork on his plate. He'd eaten three servings of eggs and bacon and could've gone for another before she'd said what she said. I figure we've got a good ten hours of drive in front of us today. Plenty of time to talk.

If you ask me, Carol said, pausing to sip her coffee, you're putting the cart in front of the horse. I don't know how you think just showing back up is enough to get me to uproot my whole life and follow you wherever it is you're going.

Wallace looked at the clock over the stove. It was twenty minutes fast, but he could still tell they were pushing it. There was probably a carload of killers making a beeline for the two of them that very minute, and if they weren't in Indiana they were probably just over the Kentucky border.

What'd you want to hear? he said. When that piece of shit did what he did, I reacted the only way I knew how. You can't blame me for that. I did what I had to do and when I looked up I had to get the hell out of town.

That's fine, she said, but what about the day after? The week after? The year after? If you cared, Bill, you would've found a way to call. You would've sent a letter. You would've snuck back and got me, like you're trying to do now.

He could hear the tick of the clock. In the cooler at his feet there came the sound of ice rustling, the head settling in. He realized he needed to buy some more ice and then he wondered what he should do with the head. Should he just leave it in the cabin and let whoever was coming find it for themselves? Leave it at a rest stop and drop Boss a quick call?

Carol snapped him back to attention. Bill, she said. You need to talk to me.

We need to leave, he said. All this nonsense, he said, we can get to later.

This isn't nonsense, she said. I'm talking about my life here. While you were busy starting a family in North Carolina, I was sitting around on my thumbs waiting on you. I don't think you understand what it was like, Bill, to have the only goddamn person in the world you love up and leave you cold like that.

Wallace picked up his plate and carried it over to the sink. He ran a stream of water over it and rinsed what was left of his breakfast down the drain. He wished he knew what word or sentence would put an end to the conversation. He wished he knew what she wanted to hear so it could be said and propel them past the whole business. For a second he wondered if there was no word, no sentence, and if this had been a bad idea to begin with. He hadn't been thinking clearly, not since he and Carp had crossed into the city limits. He'd been reacting again.

What can I say? he asked her.

Carol looked down at her plate, still populated with all of her food. I don't know, she said.

Well, he said, I don't either. Can we figure it out on the road?

Where are we going? she said.

I don't know, he said. South. West. You pick.

I don't have any interest one way or another, she said. Far as I'm concerned, I'm good as dead anyway.

Carol, he said.

One thing, she said. You tell me this and I'll pack up and leave. I'll shut up until we're a hundred miles away and I'll pick a better time to ask my questions. You answer me one thing.

Name it.

What's to keep you from leaving me again?

Wallace opened his mouth to speak. There were words bouncing in his head like ricocheting bullets – he could recognize them, their shapes, their hard angles and soft curves – but he couldn't place them or form them. He thought of Cindy, probably getting the kids ready for school that very minute. He thought of promises he'd made her. The same promises he'd made Carol. He thought of all the promises he'd ever made and realized somewhere he'd lost count. That seemed poor form to him.

I won't, he said.

Carol gave him a look he knew meant she wasn't

buying it.

The ice in the cooler rustled again.

He looked at it and then, out of the corner of his eye, he thought he saw something move out in the woods. He turned and focused and thought for sure he could see something. It was there, maybe a couple hundred yards away. Carol, he said, get the shotgun.

She sat still, unable to move.

Now, he said.

Carol leaped from her chair and ran across the living room to a closet next to the stairs leading into the basement. She pulled his shotgun from there, and as she did, she said, Bill, Bill, what's going on?

Hurry, he said and extended his hand, his eyes still trained on that spot in the woods.

She gave it to him and he took it and checked the barrels. They were both loaded and ready to go. Wallace crouched down just so his eyes were still able to peer out through the bottom edge of the window. Honey, he said to Carol, get down.

Carol lay down on her stomach on the floor. She was starting to panic, her eyes leaking tears. Bill, she said.

Shh, he said.

The shape in the woods moved again, but it was slow, patient.

Son of a bitch flew people out here, Wallace thought. Or he hired local.

He was deciding which was the better probability when there came a knock on the cabin door. Carol looked at him and her face scrunched like she was suddenly more terrified than she ever had been before. Wallace had never seen her like that and he felt awful in a way he couldn't completely comprehend.

Wasted too much time, he said to himself. Dumb, dumb, dumb.

He crept as slowly and quietly over to the door as he could in his crouch, alternating his gaze from the door to the forest. It looked like they were trying for the oldest trick in the book – the flank. More than likely they were some local toughs. Maybe moonshiners. Maybe some neo-Nazis used to pushing pills. Whoever they were, he thought, they weren't going to take their time.

The knock came again, this one louder and more persistent. Wallace was by the door, close enough to reach out and touch the knob. There was a window slot but it was decorative glass, the kind that made the person outside look like a funhouse mirror.

Wallace unlocked the knob and gently turned and pulled. He had the shotgun trained and was ready to blow away whoever burst in. He expected a charge lead by a gun barrel, a hotheaded thrust that left the attacker vulnerable. What he got was a total surprise. Standing there, his arms already up in surrender, his face stark white in shock, was Chief Dean. They both paused in a moment of recognition, the years fading away and leaving them to remember that day, long ago, when they had stood in the jailhouse together, Wallace fresh from braining Terry Wilcox and about ready to send a load of lead into Dean's knee.

They looked at each other in wordless silence, neither of them in a proper place to make a move, until one of the back windows of the cabin exploded, sending a storm of glass and wood onto the floor, a bullet passing through and landing, squarely, in Chief Dean's left shoulder and depositing him on the ground next to a stunned Wallace.

Carol screamed.

Wallace was busy working Dean's gun out of his holster. He crawled the length of the floor and peered out the window. A human shape was patiently making its way through the trees. A bullet splintered the frame a few inches away from where Wallace looked out. He dropped down and waited. When he looked back out, he saw the form again, growing closer. He could recognize him now. It was Carp coming for him, his face a mangled and bloody mess of bandages, blood all over the front of his shirt, his face the strangest mixture of expressionless and determined.

Chapter 28

The message Boss sent read, Hold grnd 3hr out. He hit the button and slid the phone back into his pocket. The plate of chicken and dumplings was still steaming in front of him. Across the booth Abel was listlessly poking at a plate of spaghetti with his fork.

You're gonna want to eat that, Boss said. Got a long ass day in front of us.

Not hungry, Abel said. Feel like I'm all hyped up.

That's normal, Boss said. Let me tell you about the first job I ever did. It was for a fella named Salmons. He was this guy down in Louisville. He used to run numbers.

Numbers? Abel said.

Gambling. Here's what you did back in the old days – you had a runner who would go from place to place, business to business, and he'd get all the money together. He'd ask people to pick a few numbers, usually three, sometimes four, and he'd get the money. All of it went into this big pool and you spun a wheel or picked out some pieces of paper for a lottery.

How long ago was this?

Forty, forty-five years ago. I was just getting started. I was, uh, he looked around the diner at the few people populating the booths, at Simmons and a bruised Lucrow across the way, wet behind the ears.

The phone vibrated in his pocket and he pulled it

out and looked at it. Fine, it said. 3 in the house. Cop.

Cop, Boss said. Jesus Christ.

What? Abel said.

Boss typed the keys on his phone and sent a message that read, Isolated?

Anyway, he said and put the phone on the table, there was a guy back then, his name was Murray, and Murray was a real no-good bastard. Used to hold people up all the time. Didn't matter if you knew Murray, he'd still pull a gun and take everything in your pocket. Got to the point where somebody would get robbed and you'd say, goddamn Murray again without even knowing the specifics.

How'd he get away with it?

He didn't, Boss said and looked at his phone. Yes, the new message read. Isolated. The point is, Boss said, Salmons got tired of it. He was a cranky old fella anyway. Used to walk around talking about his hemorrhoids all the time. He'd have a meeting and you'd have to all gather, maybe ten of you, in the bathroom and he'd be there soaking his hemorrhoids in the tub.

Abel looked down at his spaghetti and then dropped his fork. Nice, he said.

I told you, Boss said, eat up. Boss picked up his own fork and shoveled a few dumplings into his mouth. Then a few more. His plate was nearly cleaned by the time Abel started in again. So Salmon was there in his bathtub, Boss said, and he looks at me and he says, Valentine, you're up. I about shit my pants, Abel. I didn't know Salmons knew my name. I didn't think anybody did. And being up was big. It meant it was time to handle your business.

So what was the business?

The business was taking a golf club, Boss said, a three iron if I remember right, and going down and finding Murray and breaking his fucking arm.

You do it?

Yeah, I did it. It was my turn. I kicked in his door and that son of a bitch pulled a piece and I was running on adrenaline and I swung that club and knocked it out of his hand and then got to work breaking his arm.

Abel poked at his mound of spaghetti and shook his head. His complexion was pale.

You gonna get sick on me? Boss said.

No, Abel said. I'm just new to this.

No shit, Boss said. That's what I'm saying. You may be new, but that doesn't mean your turn's not coming.

What if I don't want my turn?

Well, Boss said, you either want it or you don't. If you don't, I'd suggest you get on the first bus back to Carolina. You want that?

Abel shook his head slowly. I don't think so, he said.

Good, Boss said. Long as you know.

They finished eating and Boss and Abel and Simmons and Lucrow paid their bills and went outside to the parking lot. Boss' car was parked on the other side of the lot, but before he got in he went over to the U-Haul van and talked to Simmons.

We're in for the rest of the haul, he said. That good with you fellas?

Sure thing, Simmons said. Good with you? he said to Lucrow.

Lucrow shrugged. He looked haunted in a way, his face still battered and swollen. Sure, he said.

Good, Boss said. Hey, he said, you hear that?

They listened for a moment. There was the whine of tractor-trailers hitting their air brakes as they came off the highway. Then it was a bit more audible. Muffled sounds. Sounds like mouths bound with rags and tape trying to make themselves heard.

Sounds to me like your furniture's tired of being on the road, Boss said with a smile.

Simmons forced himself to grin and said, You bet.

Oh well, Boss said and banged on the door to the U-Haul. Still got lots of miles to cover.

Boss walked back to his car and got inside. Abel was fiddling with the dials on the radio. You want me to put another one on? he said and lifted his phone.

No, Boss said. Let's get some news on here. He turned the dial until he found a station that played regular news updates. He said, I'm in the mood to know just how the world's doing. Let's see if there's anything interesting cooking in the Hoosier state.

Chapter 29

Something about the way Wallace's wife held his head reminded Dean of when he was little. He'd taken a fever once – my God, the voice said to him, remember how it burned – and the damn thing had just grown and grown and grown until everything was sweat and delusions. All he could recollect was the ceiling of his grandmama's spare bedroom and his mama's face hovering over him, a wet washrag covering his eyes from time to time.

It happens, his grandmama had said three days into the ordeal. You get a little one that young and they catch it and they burn up. Like a candle, she said.

No, his mama said, working that washrag. No, no, no, no, no, he's gonna be just fine. Ain't you, honey?

I don't know, Dean said.

What's that? Wallace's wife said, leaning closer. What'd you say, Chief?

Carol, Wallace said from across the room, be quiet.

I said I don't know about that, Dean said.

Shut him up, Wallace said.

I think he's coming to, she said. I keep telling you, we need to use that radio. Get somebody up here.

Let it alone. I'm looking at life right now. Worse.

Life's better than death, Wallace's wife said and brushed Dean's hair off his forehead.

That's a hell of a way to put it, Dean thought to

himself. Back then, as a boy, he'd found himself wishing for death in a fashion that would've terrified his mama and his preacher. The fever had been so hot, so nasty, that sometimes he'd wake up in the middle of the night, fresh off a swirl of hallucinations filled with the devil's face – was it that man's face, the broken skull outside with the obliterated mouth, or was it just that way now, how he was remembering it now with the round deep in his shoulder? – and he'd pray, pray and beg, to whatever god might be listening, Take me, take me, Jesus God take me, please, have mercy and just make it end.

He closed his eyes to rest. Is he coming? a woman's voice said.

You bet your ass he's coming, Dean said. For the bible tells us so.

No, Wallace answered. He's just standing there.

What's he want?

Salvation, Dean said.

His mama was standing over him, whispering, late in the night, Darlin', you're the most precious thing in my life. Darlin', darlin', darlin' boy, the most precious thing God ever brought into my life, praise Him and the Son.

Dean reached blindly for his gun and found his holster empty.

They went and took it, the voice said.

You took my piece? he said.

I'm sorry, Wallace's wife whispered. I'm so damn sorry about this, Chief. Her voice was tired, choked with tears. We're gonna get through this now, so you hold on.

178

Hold on. His mama had said that too.

He's just standing there, Wallace said. What in the fuck is he waiting on?

Dean opened his eyes. He saw Wallace crouched against the wall, the shotgun poised. The wound in his shoulder was alive, a great fire burning. Felt like half his body had been sheered off. He turned his head slowly, deliberately, and saw Wallace's wife reaching across him and holding a shirt against the wound. He'd seen her in a grocery store, maybe two weeks before, in the frozen food aisle. It was like she'd aged twenty years since then.

Stay down, the voice told him. Stay down, you old fart.

Maybe, he said to it.

He's waking up, the woman said.

Keep him down, Wallace said.

Dean surveyed the room. A nice cabin, dusty though. The window had exploded. He remembered that. There was blood and glass littering the floor. In the kitchen he could see where they'd been having breakfast. Plates, glasses, mugs. Under the table a red and white cooler. It confused the hell out of him. It didn't seem to fit there. Seemed out of place. Maybe they were packing up to take off and bringing some food with them. Maybe they had some things to keep cold.

Maybe ...

I'll be goddamned, he said.

Just die already, the voice said. This ain't got nothing to do with you and it's gonna get a good sight messier before it's all said and done. Clock out and say goodnight, it said.

Shut up, you pussy, Dean said.

What's he saying? Wallace said.

He's talking gibberish, Carol said.

The fuck I am, Dean said. Bill Wallace, he said, you son of a bitch. He sat up and took a breath of air that rattled around in his chest and only served to make the pain in his shoulder sing louder. Tell me you don't have Yorkie Goodman's goddamn head in that there goddamn cooler.

Wallace looked at him. His lips pursed and he whistled. When the tune ended he wiped some sweat off his brow and smiled, Chief, he said, I'd be more than happy to tell you that, but I ain't much of a liar.

Chapter 30

The army surplus store was in an old Taco Bell building that Boss had been in twenty years before. He'd stopped there with his ex-wife Betty on their way into Nashville to ski for the weekend. As he was walking in with Abel and his men, he stopped and shook his head. The trip had been a disaster. The weather hadn't cooperated and the snow that'd been forecast never made it, leaving Boss and Betty to spend the whole time holed up in a stuffy room in the Nashville Inn. Every night they went downstairs and had dinner in the restaurant and somehow or another there was always a fight. On the drive back to Seymour they'd finally put into words what'd been brewing for so very long.

You all right? Abel asked him.

You bet, Boss said. Just remembering something.

What?

Nothing important, he said and reached for the door.

The store was lit by fluorescents that buzzed loudly and threw a yellow tint onto all the shelves and the various canteens and ammo boxes stacked haphazardly. Directly ahead, sitting behind a glass case full of gas masks and bayonets, was a middle-aged man wearing a wife-beater and sporting a dramatic white combover. Howdy, he said as Boss and his crew walked up. What can I do for you boys?

You Russell? Boss said.

You bet, the man said. And if I ain't, I need to get to work on ordering new checks.

Good, Boss said. We're friends of Larry Newman.

Russell nodded as he stood out of his chair. I heard y'all were coming through. You wanna follow me into the back?

He left his post at the display case and led them through a set of swinging doors and into what had, once upon a time, been the kitchen. There were still stainless steel sinks and an assembly line where the workers had put together their orders, but the shelves and recesses were filled with boxes of bullets, banana clips, gun oils, sights, and straps. Toward the back were three large boxes clearly labeled FATIGUES in red-stenciled letters.

These came in 'bout an hour ago, Russell said. You boys are welcome to whatever you want.

Boss' men pulled out box cutters and opened the packages. In the first box were a half dozen AKMs and an assortment of clips. Simmons looked at one and said, You didn't tell us we were going Russian for this one.

They sent what they had, Boss said.

Nah, Russell said, that there's a good one. A classic. Say, he said, it ain't one damn bit any of my business, but what the hell you guys out here for? Hunting rhino?

You got it, Boss said. Hunting rhino.

Huh, Russell said. I feel sorry for that sonuvabitch.

Abel left Boss' side and looked into the second

box. Shakily, he pulled out a pump-action. He held it and turned pale. Hey, he said to Boss, is this a good one?

Boss took the shotgun from him and pumped it. Sure, he said, but what we're doing here isn't gonna need the kind of kick a shotgun gives you. Hey, Boss said to the young man, you got any pieces in there?

The young man handed Boss a Grand Power K100. He leveled it and looked down the barrel.

Here, he said and gave it to Abel. A piece is gonna serve you a hell of a lot better. Shotgun's messy, can get messier if we're up close or in a tight space. This thing? he said and pointed at the K100, that's gonna be all you need.

Abel turned the gun around in his hands and examined it. All right, he said.

If it suits y'all, Russell said, I'm gonna leave you be for awhile and sit out front. Don't need to hear more than I've already heard.

Hold on, Boss said. Tell me something.

Name it.

You got any bangs?

Russell scratched his cheek and darted his eyes about the room. Let's see what we can scrounge up.

Boss followed Russell into the next room over. It was a former manager's office that reeked of smoke and had a desk pushed up against a wall. The desk itself was covered in discarded papers and torn envelopes and the walls were papered with political cartoons. One that caught Boss' eye was a picture of the Statue of Liberty holding an AK-47. Bloody letters under her read WE'LL BE READY NEXT TIME.

Tell you what, Russell said and rifled through a drawer in the desk, this here is from my own stock. He produced a flashbang that had the words FUCK YOU painted in Wite-Out on the side. Newman told me y'all were good folks, so you can have one on me.

That's mighty kind, Boss said.

Sure thing, Russell said. Newman told me how you took care of those little twats round Indy. Told me all about it.

Boss read the side of the flashbang again.

FUCK YOU.

Okay, Russell said, throwing his hands up, I've gotta get back to the store. You and your boys have at whatever you want. It's on the house, far as I'm concerned.

Boss stuffed the flashbang into his pocket and reached out to shake Russell's hand. We'll be out of your hair in a minute or two, he said.

You got it, Russell said. Get what you need and go kill the fuck out of that rhino.

Done and done, Boss said.

Chapter 31

There was a woodpile a good twenty feet away from the rear of the cabin. Carp had maneuvered his way there and half-squatted and half-laid across it, using a decent-sized log between for cover. He had a clear line of sight to the window of the main room of the cabin. In order for Wallace to get a shot, he would have to peek up and over the windowsill, giving Carp the perfect angle to cut him off. It had been a half an hour since the last round was fired and it was simply a matter of keeping vigilant.

The phone buzzed in his pocket and he slipped it out without taking his eyes off the cabin. He brought the screen up to eye-level and read the text, 10 min.

He saw a shadow move inside the cabin. It was probably Wallace rushing from one room of the cabin to another. Maybe his wife panicking. Carp was almost certain the Chief was either dead or just this side of it.

Carp, a voice yelled from the cabin. Carp, you can have the head.

Before he answered, he focused on the window from which the voice had originated. The broken glass and frame made it look like a giant, rabid mouth was chewing its way out of the cabin. That's not good enough, Carp yelled back.

There was silence except for a brisk wind that had kicked up in the woods somewhere and then rolled through. The bandage and gauze on Carp's face rustled and it suddenly occurred to him to remove it. The thought was as simple and elementary as any thought he'd ever entertained. It was like thinking about walking across a room. He reached with his free hand and loosened the strips of tape and peeled the bandage off. When he did he looked down at it and saw there were ribbons of skin and flesh hanging off, colored black and seemingly hot. Bits of bone like grit dotted the bandage.

It all seemed foreign to Carp, like something that was happening to someone else. The pain had been absent since his vision earlier, but there was still a throbbing present, an echo of hurt that rested where his jaw had once been.

Tell me what you want, Wallace called to him.

Carp looked up from the bandage and back at the cabin. He could see the barrel of Wallace's shotgun rising from the bottom of the window like an antenna. I want you to wait, Carp yelled back with considerable difficulty. I want you to see what comes next.

Chapter 32

Behind Wallace the Chief said, We've got company.

Wallace crab-walked across the floor to where Carol and the Chief were ducked down. Through a window by the door he saw the U-Haul and Boss' car rolling up the driveway. He heard the pop of the gravel under the wheels and a surge of adrenaline flooded through him. Carol, he said, get the Chief upstairs.

Bill, she said.

Now, he said.

Carol helped Dean to his feet and the two of them hobbled over to the base of the stairs. Bill, Dean said, give me a gun.

Chief, Wallace said, you're more than likely to shoot me.

True, Dean said, but if it's just the same to you, I'll wait 'til this shitstorm of a mess is done and settled before I do it.

That sounded good to Wallace and he handed Dean back his piece.

Carol, he said, pausing to look into her eyes. There was nothing but fear and hurt there and studying it too long made him feel as lowdown as he ever thought he could feel. He said, I'm sorry.

She chose not to answer and moved with Dean up the stairs, taking each one carefully until they were up in the loft with the bedrooms. When they were tucked away, Wallace looked back out the window and saw Boss, Abel, and two of Boss' men gathering at the rear of the U-Haul. They were all packing semi-automatics. Boss seemed as large as an oversized statue, a colossus towering over the rest of his crew.

Wallace watched him talk with the men and direct them. The younger man hustled off around the cabin, more than likely to join Carp, while the older one kept watch on the front of the cabin. Wallace knew it was a no-win situation and thought briefly about just turning the shotgun on himself. It seemed a decent option, but then he remembered Carol upstairs.

Wait, he thought, remembering her and then Cindy and the kids. And what the hell is in that truck?

Boss was standing nonchalantly next to it, a champion of a smile working its way across his pudgy face. Wallace recognized it immediately. It was the smile of a man holding all the right cards.

Chapter 33

The first out of the truck was Cindy, a black hood over her head, her wrists bound with tape. She wore a pale blue sweatshirt that Wallace instantly recognized. Behind her, the boy and the girl in pajamas, their small bodies hunched over, cold, shaking, frightened.

Boss didn't bother to watch them being unloaded. Instead he stood with his back to them, his beefy arms crossed over his chest. He checked his watch and then called Wallace on his phone.

When Wallace answered, Boss said, Hello, Bill.

What? Wallace said. What do you want?

I'm sending Lucrow up to the porch. Give him the head and we'll go from there.

When Boss gave him the signal, Lucrow approached the cabin, his steps careful and measured. Before the front door cracked, he looked back at Simmons, hesitant, waiting for the go-ahead. When the door opened slightly, Lucrow peeked inside. From his vantage point Boss could see movement inside. Lucrow reaching for something. A shotgun boomed and Lucrow's lifeless body flopped to the porch.

Abel, standing to Boss' side, yelled Fuck and nearly dropped his piece.

Boss dialed Wallace's number. You fuckhead. You've got one more chance, he said and snapped his fingers. Abel came to him and Boss pointed at Carol.

He went to her and pressed his gun against her hooded head. Yorkie's head, Boss said, or your wife eats it.

Simmons took his turn next, climbing the steps cautiously to the porch, taking great care to step around his partner's body. As he reached for the door knob he kept his rifle leveled. When Wallace handed him the red cooler, Simmons took it and backed quickly away from the cabin. He brought it to Boss and set it at his feet. Before Boss could open it, his phone buzzed.

You got the head, Wallace spit. Let's call it even.

Oh, Boss said, I don't know if I'd go that far.

Boss, Wallace said, one dad to another, please.

Boss heard the crack of a window breaking in the rear of the cabin. Wallace yelled, What the fuck, over the phone and then Boss saw the explosion of the flashbang inside as he put his phone away.

Carp emerged from the front door, dragging Wallace by his shirt. He deposited him in the dirt next to the cooler and pistol-whipped him for good measure.

Howdy Carp, Boss said.

Carp said something, his wreck of a jaw opening with a sick cracking sound, his tongue a loose animal.

Oh God, Abel said, is he going to die?

Can't say you haven't looked better, Boss said to him.

Carp emitted another mash of sounds, but was interrupted as Wallace, his face buried in the dust, stirred and moaned. With the tip of his oxford, Boss rolled him over onto his back and pointed his rifle at his head.

Wallace, Boss said, you cannot say I didn't give you fair warning.

More than I deserved, Wallace said with a groan.

You got that right, Boss said. But here's the deal.

No deal, Wallace said. Go ahead and do what you got to do. Leave Carol and Cindy and the kids out of it. They got no part in any of this.

You made them a part of it, Boss said.

They did nothing wrong.

They associated themselves with your waste-of-space ass, Wallace.

Boss.

Don't Boss me, son, he said, squatting down. You put this situation in motion. You hear that boy over there crying? You hear that wife and daughter of yours shivering? That's you. You did that. He looked at Abel and Abel cocked his gun.

Cindy began to beg, her voice a stream of please, please, please.

Boss frowned as if what he was about to say truly troubled him. You taught her that language, Wallace. You introduced this tragedy into her life.

Cindy, he said.

Now, Boss said, before I spray your brains all over the ground, you got a choice to make. Way I see it, it's a choice you've had coming a while now.

No, Wallace said. Please.

It's either the pretty lady you got in the house, Boss said, or it's this here darlin' and your little ones. Better get to thinking because the clock starts running now.

Chapter 34

Carol was huddled in the corner and sobbing so loud Dean thought she might burst. Hey, he said to her, still holding his bleeding shoulder, you need to calm down, hon. You need to take a breath.

It's either the pretty lady you got in the house, he heard Boss say outside, or it's this here darlin' and the little ones.

Shitfire, Dean said to himself.

They're gonna kill me, Carol said between sobs.

No ma'am, Dean said to her and scooted across the floor. Hon, he said, you got a weapon up here? Anything with a sight on it?

Carol's crying stopped momentarily and she craned her neck to stare at the ceiling. Chief, she said, I knew this was a bad idea.

Sure you did, Dean said. Sure you did.

He ain't the best man in the world, she said, but I loved him.

I know it, Dean said. Hon, I need something. I need a weapon of some sort.

He paused in his scooting and heard the family outside crying.

Hon, Dean said, his voice strengthening and taking on the tone he'd learned to use when settling a dispute, I need you to focus now.

Chief, she said.

Hon, he said. I need a rifle. And fast.

For a moment she gathered herself and crawled over to a set of drawers across from the bed. They were handmade pieces of furniture, one of the few things her father the Judge ever spent his hard-earned money on. When she reached for the handle to open a drawer, the sound it made was true and strong, the note of a piece of art.

Dean watched the woman pull a Browning A-Bolt out of the drawer. Holding it, her hands trembling, she said, It's Bill's.

That's fine, Dean said. Can I have it?

Here, she said and held it out.

Dean scooted closer and took the rifle.

We used to shoot bottles with it, she said.

Uh huh, Dean said and checked to make sure there was a bullet in the chamber.

Used to go out in the country, she said, her voice betraying her.

Dean looked down the sight and cursed the gun momentarily for not having a scope attached. The voice whispered to him, goddamn cheap sonuvabitch, and Dean quietly told it to simmer down.

Oh God, Carol said. Oh God, oh God, oh God.

Shh, Dean said. Stay right there. Don't have the slightest idea yet how this thing's going to work out.

With great effort he scooted back to his spot beneath the upstairs window and hazarded himself to peek outside. Wallace was still on the ground, the big man's foot planted squarely on his chest and aiming a piece at his face. To his side was the family, all of them on their knees, all of them shaking. That monster with half a face was with the boy now, both of them waiting.

Come on now, the big man said. We ain't got all day, Bill.

Dean got up on his haunches and opened the window the slightest bit. When it was done he got the barrel of the rifle in place and looked down the fixed sight. His options were limited, he knew that, but he still had them.

Say, the voice said to him, what're you fixing to do here?

Exactly what I learned to do, he said.

Yeah, the voice said, then what?

No idea.

You ain't sniped in years.

Shut up.

Dean closed one eye and squinted the other. First he got his hairs on the big man, but then he travelled down his arm and his gun and came to Wallace's face. Dean could see over the barrel where Wallace's lips were pursing, working toward formulating an answer.

He's in a no-win situation.

No shit, Dean said to the voice.

You reckon this is about revenge or mercy?

Ain't they the same thing? Dean said.

Before the voice could respond Dean squeezed the trigger of the rifle and hoped that somewhere, deep down, he really knew the difference.

Chapter 35

The round from the rifle hit true and with a crack of thunder took the question from Wallace. As it did, everyone on the lawn flinched.

Boss.

Carp and Abel with their sights on Cindy and the kids.

Cindy and the kids.

Simmons, who had been considering high-tailing it out of there anyway.

Carol, who was over in the corner, bracing herself.

Who was it? she asked Chief Dean.

Never mind, he said and got low to the floor.

Carp reacted first by returning fire to the second floor window of the cabin. He fired a half dozen shots before his clip emptied. Then ran for cover behind the U-Haul. Waiting for him there was Abel, who had crawled under the bumper and abandoned his gun.

After the first few shots from Carp, Dean expected what was left of the crew to make their way into the cabin and up the stairs. He had a few rounds left in his revolver, but by his calculations he would only take out one, two if he was lucky, before somebody overwhelmed him and the woman. He cinched up against the wall facing the stairs and waited with the hammer cocked.

Nobody came.

When he worked up the courage, he looked out

the window again. The sill was splintered from one of Carp's rounds and he gripped the wood carefully as he lifted himself up. Outside, the men stood around the area where he'd shot Wallace, where Wallace's lifeless body lay now, just a heap of skin and bone and muscle and blood. But they were tending to the big man. He was down to the side of Wallace, in the gore, his hands resting over his chest as his face turned a violent shade of red.

Fat sonuvabitch is having a heart attack, Dean thought.

The man missing half his face and the other older man worked together to drag the big man and the dead guy on the porch over to where the car was parked. They loaded them into the back seat. The boy, who had been hiding beneath the U-Haul, scurried over and took the keys. When he got the car started, he spun its tires in the dirt. The kid's panicking, Dean thought. After the older man got in the passenger seat, the car sped in reverse down the driveway, narrowly avoiding careening off into the gorge behind the cabin.

Only the man missing half his face remained. He walked calmly back to the scene and Dean watched him study the mess that Wallace had become. With the tip of his boot he moved around bits of what was left of him and then looked up at the window. At first Dean expected more gunfire and ducked back. When it didn't come, he edged his way to the window again and saw the man was still gazing up in his direction. His face was such a gnarled travesty now that it was as if it was dissolving in real time, fragments of him disintegrating as the birds in the woods twittered and sang. The man reached up with his hand and first brushed away another segment of his flesh, squeezing it in his fist. Blood and gore leaked out from between his knuckles and then, meeting Dean's eyes, he loosened his grip and the blood and skin slipped from his fingers and dripped onto the grass. Next, as if it was the logical thing to do, with a great twisting and tugging, he wrestled from his skull the last remaining chunk of his jaw, a piece of white bone that, had Dean come across it on a walk, he might've thought belonged to a dead animal. The man knelt with it in his hand, the jawbone, and placed it ever so delicately atop Wallace's now-still chest.

Without another wasted movement, the man picked up the handle of the red and white cooler. After quickly regarding the hooded and restrained family, the three of them in a writhing huddle on the ground, the children nesting next to their mother, their chests heaving, he carried the cooler to the U-Haul, climbed into the cab, started the engine, and simply drove away.

Is it over? Carol asked from the corner.

Maybe, Dean said. God help us, I hope so.

Chapter 36

Bockwinkel sat with Jimmy Lee in the jail and examined his cards. Low spades. Deuce, four, five, six, nine between his two draws.

You gonna look all day or make a bid?

Jimmy Lee, he said, if you're gonna get smart, I'd prefer to go on and fold.

Nothin' smart, Jimmy Lee said and thumbed his cards. Just worse than playin' with an old blue-hair.

Three, Bockwinkel said.

Three total?

Three total, he said. That's more than enough.

On the desk a few feet away, Bockwinkel's walkie-talkie squawked as a call came through. Bockwinkel got up and twisted the volume down. It was no doubt another call from out at the crime scene at Yorkie Goodman's and he had no intention of heading that way again. They could fire him. He'd decided, that'd be just fine. He'd rather go and work for his father-in-law and handle parking lot security on the weekends at the Sur-Way than take another look at that mess.

Ain't you got work? Jimmy Lee asked him.

Ain't you got a lead to throw?

Jimmy Lee sucked on his teeth before throwing an ace of clubs.

I know it's strategy, Bockwinkel said, but Grandpa Bockwinkel always told us it was low-class to lead the game with an ace.

I'm guessin' Grandpa Bockwinkel didn't win spades too often.

Nah, Bockwinkel said and threw a five. Reckon he didn't.

The phone rang then and Bockwinkel got up again and grabbed the receiver. He very nearly picked it up and put it right back down, but Chief Dean had been gone the better part of the day and might be checking in. On the other end though was the office's liaison with the State Police.

Dean there? he said.

No sir, Bockwinkel said. Stepped out awhile.

The trooper cursed under his breath. I got to ask, he said, y'all do any work in Seymour?

Not if we can help it.

You get Dean on the horn the second he gets in.

How about the second after? Bockwinkel asked him. Figure that first one he'll be busy closing the door behind him.

The trooper hung up and Bockwinkel couldn't help but smile. The State boys had been pricks since they'd swept in and taken over the office the day before, ordering everyone around like they owned the place. Way Bockwinkel figured, if they wanted to act like the SPD was a bunch of backward hicks and take over the scene at Yorkie's and the hotel, then they were sure as hell gonna get a bunch of backward hicks.

I tell you what, Jimmy Lee said as Bockwinkel sat back down, you got a super-sized bug up your ass.

Bockwinkel watched him throw the king of clubs and then slapped down his Jack. You know what I make? he asked Jimmy Lee.

What's that?

Thirty. Thirty thousand dollars. For that kind of money I'm more than willin' to go in and deal with drunks like your dumb ass or stop a beatin' or two.

Thirty thousand, Jimmy Lee said and laid down a king of hearts. Jesus. My cousin makes more than that at the Lowe's in Terre Haute.

You want me to go pokin' around a headless body? Bockwinkel whistled. I'm gonna need at least thirty-five.

The two were chuckling as a car door slammed outside, causing Bockwinkel to jump up and look out the window. He saw the Chief helping a pair of woman and a pair of kids out of his parked cruiser. Bockwinkel hurried out to help and saw that Dean's uniform was soaked through with blood.

Chief, he said, shit, you all right?

I've been better, Dean said with a grimace. For now, just get these here people inside.

The women and children were hurried into the jail and Bockwinkel got them into the pair of waiting cells as Dean pulled shut all the blinds and Jimmy Lee sat with his cards and watched.

I got to get ahold of State, Dean said as he went to his desk. Bockwinkel, you make sure all the doors are locked and we got some arms. Jimmy Lee?

Yeah?

You are hereby deputized.

Jimmy Lee sat up straight in his chair and smiled. You for real, Chief?

Dean had his phone up to his ear already. Jimmy

Lee, he said, I ain't got time to bullshit around.

Bockwinkel gathered up what guns and ammo they had in the office, including all the SWAT shotguns and the semi-automatics the state had sent three years prior and had been sitting and collecting dust in the arms locker. He piled all of the ammunition on his desk and rounds went skittering off onto the floor and he was down on his knees and collecting them, the world moving fast now, reaching under chairs and desks long since unused for bullets and then he heard the children sobbing in the cell and he looked up and saw them staring at him with big glassy eyes that were bloodshot and trembling.

Hey, he said to them. It's okay. It's okay.

He looked to the mother, a pretty woman in a blood-splattered blue sweatshirt. It seemed like she was out of place, like she didn't belong in that cell. When they met eyes, he meant to let her know they were safe, that the children needn't cry, but what he got back in return was so awful and terrible he couldn't look anymore.

Chief, Bockwinkel said. They need an ambulance?

No, Dean said, it's not their blood. Then, into the phone, Nashville. Judge's Quarters. That's right. Uh huh. One body. Uh huh.

Hey, Bockwinkel said to the children again, this time noticing their wrists were red and scraped and showed marks from where they'd been tied. It's going to be okay.

The Chief said, We need backup here, just in case, and hung up the phone. He gestured for a gun. Bockwinkel left the family in the cell and handed

Dean one of the rifles. The Chief took it and locked in a clip. Bockwinkel, he said, prying open the blinds and searching, be ready for just about anything.

Sure, Bockwinkel said.

Jimmy Lee started to speak and Bockwinkel put up a finger to hush him.

It was quiet then as Dean kept an eye out the window and Bockwinkel stood at his side and waited for whatever might be coming. There was the occasional sound of the furnace trying to kick on and failing, a car driving past on the street, but save for that and the low crying of the children, it was silent until the woman from one cell, the one without the little ones, walked carefully out of her cell door and into the other cell. Bockwinkel turned long enough to see the woman lower herself to her knees and reach out to the mother with her arms. Though Bockwinkel had thought he'd noticed some unspoken tension between them, something unresolved, the mother leaned into the other woman and the two women and the little boy and the little girl came together and held one another like a family long since separated.

Chapter 37

Carp, Simmons said. Carp, you good back there? He looked into the backseat where Carp was lying with his head wrapped in a beehive of gauze and resting on a stack of pillows. The blood and pus had worn through and into the pillows. For long stretches of the drive, he'd taken glimpses in the rearview, each time hoping to hell he'd see Carp's chest moving.

I don't know, Allen, his new partner, said. I don't like this.

Hey, Simmons said, if there's one motherfucker who can kick this thing, it's the man in the backseat.

The car moved from asphalt to dirt and the front passenger-side tire dipped into a significant hole and rocked the car. From the backseat, and through the gauze, came a low moan.

Ah, Simmons said. Evening, Carp.

He groaned.

Almost home. Just hang tight.

Hey, Allen whispered. Is it as bad as everyone was saying?

Simmons took his eyes off the dirt road for a moment and caught Allen's. He nodded and mouthed the word yes.

Christ, Allen said.

They passed a gate and Simmons leaned into the wheel and squinted his eyes. How many gates is that?

I have no idea, Allen said.

No? Simmons said. You ain't got one of those photographic memories then?

Allen gave him a look like he'd lost it. No, he said. Is that shit real?

From what I hear, Simmons said and turned the car sharply into the next gate on the right. He saw the burnt-out cars and knew he'd found the right driveway. The sun was still low in the sky and the red light leaked out over the property and the rust on the cars seemed to positively glow.

Eerie, Allen said.

You ain't seen nothin' yet, Simmons said.

The two men helped Carp out of the car, looping his arms over their shoulders and practically carrying him up onto the porch and through the door. Simmons directed his new partner to deposit Carp in the recliner in the living room and then retrieved two pairs of gloves from the bathroom. Next, he pulled an IV stand from the closet and set it with a bag of blood and then searched through the totes on the floor for morphine. With it came a quick instruction manual and he carried that into the living room too.

Here, he said and handed the manual to Allen. Walk me through it.

Allen took the booklet but when Simmons was ready to begin he was silent.

You okay? he said.

No, Allen said. I don't think so.

All right, Simmons said. That's to be expected. This ain't the easiest job in the world.

He took the manual back from Allen and told him to go and get some air. Without argument, Allen walked back to the door and paused long enough to get another peek at the man sitting in the recliner. The boys at the gym had been buzzing all day about him.

That sonuvabitch doesn't feel pain, they said.

Got the whole side of his face blown off, another said, and it didn't slow him down one bit.

Allen stood on the porch and pulled a Camel from his pack and lit it with shaking hands and took a long and deep drag. His lungs rang like a bell and he felt himself calm if only for a moment. Out in the yard were the burnt-out cars. With the sun disappearing over the horizon now, they were dark shapes against the dying sky.

He checked his watch. Seven eighteen. The surgeon from Charlotte was due at eight-thirty. He got back up and looked through the window that led to the front room. Simmons had the IVs set up and there were plastic tubes running down to Carp's arm. The gauze around his face, the beehive, was being unwound by Simmons and, though he knew better, Allen kept watching. Each layer, as it came off, felt like a tick on a clock to him and as it got to the last stretch he told himself again to look away but ignored the good advice.

As the final strip came loose, he fell back on the porch and screamed. The cry he released was like the sound a child might make in a haunted house or as a playmate jumped from the shadows. He tried to cap it but had as much luck as he had had in making himself stop watching. Within seconds Simmons came running out the door.

Shut the fuck up, he said. You don't know who

you're fucking with.

Fuck, Allen said. That's so ...

Shut up, Simmons said again. That's one guy you don't want to rile up.

As Simmons went back into the house to finish changing Carp's dressings, Allen crawled off of the porch and then sprinted toward the car. It felt like something was coming for him, stalking him in the new night, but when he turned, all he saw was the stubborn silhouette of the cars.

Then it was like the stalking was from the other direction and he looked and saw the burning of the light in the house. He thought of what he'd seen there. The graying skin. The milky eyes rolling wildly and independently inside the man's sockets. His head a death's head. The space where there should've been a lower set of teeth, jaw, chin, but now only a window to a neck covered in clotting and still-slick blood. A white tongue lashing the air like a snake searching for home.

Allen, he heard Simmons call from the house, if you've got your shit together, I need some help here.

He dropped his cigarette and stamped it out. A small flurry of sparks flew into the dirt and disappeared. He knew he had two options. There were always two, somebody had said to him somewhere along the way. You stay, they said, or you get the hell out. He looked at the house and the burning light and then back to the many, many miles of dark and unknown earth surrounding him.

Chapter 38

Did you bring it? Boss asked.

Abel moved nearer to his bed. I brought it, he said.

Good boy, Boss said. The incessant beeping of the machines in his hospital room spoke for a moment while he gathered his breath. I'm proud of you, he said.

Thanks, Abel said, his voice wavering.

You did good, he said.

Thanks.

How is your mother?

Not the best. She told me to tell you she's sorry she hasn't come.

She's sensitive, Boss said. It was hard for him now to keep his focus. Sometimes the drugs seeped in like an unexpected rain and left him feeling damp and slow. So sensitive, he said.

What do you want me to do? Abel asked.

Bring it up here, Boss said. Please.

Boss closed his eyes and tried to conserve enough strength. He opened them when he felt the weight of the cooler on the bed at his side.

I'm sorry, Abel said, near tears.

You don't have to be sorry. There's nothing to be sorry about.

I guess, he said, but I'm still sorry.

Stop, Boss said. There's no need for sorry

anymore. Open it, please.

He watched through his blurry vision as Abel opened the cooler.

There's police outside, Abel said. They're in the lobby. One in the waiting area.

They talk to you?

Not much, he said. They watch mostly.

They don't have anything then, Boss said.

Okay, Abel said.

Abel, Boss said. I can't see.

What do you need? Abel said.

Wet a rag, Boss said and waited while Abel wet a rag. Rub it against my eyes. Abel did as he was asked and soon the world came to Boss in clearer vision and the color of the cooler now was fire engine red. Thank you, son.

Now what? Abel said.

Lift it up for me, Boss said.

He watched Abel survey the room. Should I lock the door?

Yes, Boss said. If that makes you feel better.

It does.

He waited again while Abel locked the room. All right, he said. Show me.

Boss closed his eyes again and listened to the rumble of ice moving and falling. He opened them and staring back was the washed-out head of Yorkie Goodman. The skin was like soggy paper and the eyes cast down and staring mournfully at Boss' feet and the lips drawn as if they belonged to some great and tragic clown.

Yorkie, Boss said. You old piece of shit.

What now? Abel said.

Well, Boss said, it's your turn, Abel.

Wait, he said.

There is no waiting, Boss said. It's your turn. That's how this works.

What're you trying to say?

Hold it for me, Boss said. And flip off the machines.

I can't, Abel said.

You can, Boss said. Please.

I can't, Abel said again.

Abel, he said. It's your turn.

Now Abel did as he was asked and while holding the head he reached behind Boss and pulled as many cords from the crowd of machines as he could bunch in his fist. As he did, water from the head dripped on the floor and bed and Boss' face and Abel took the rag again and wiped Boss' clammy forehead.

Bring him down here again, Boss said.

Okay, Abel said. I'm sorry.

You don't need to be sorry.

I'm sorry I wasn't what you wanted.

But you are, Boss said weakly. Don't worry, son. You are.

The head came into Boss' vision again as his body panicked from the sudden lack of assistance. The strength was leeching from him now and his vision grew cloudy and unsure. He kept staring though, right into those dead eyes, and as he slipped under, he found himself back on the sunlit playground of Seymour Elementary, cowering below the looming, damning figure of Yorkie Goodman as he came nearer with clenched fists.

He remembered then how Yorkie had blocked out the sun as he straddled him and rained down blow after blow. How his stomach roiled and burned and then evacuated itself like an animal begging for mercy it knew full and well would never come. And again he felt the white-hot anger as Yorkie finally stood and walked away, arm-in-arm with his conspirators, leaving him in the grass to stare at the boiling fire in the sky overhead. Then it returned to him, the complete and indescribable peace he had felt only that once, the calm that had washed over him as he'd made himself a promise and knew beyond doubt that something had forever changed, that life, wherever it would go and whatever it would become, was only just beginning.

END

About the Author

Rowdy Yates

A born-and-bred Hoosier, Rowdy Yates (Jared Yates Sexton) is an expat working as an Assistant Professor of Creative Writing at Georgia Southern University. Since earning his MFA from Southern Illinois University in 2008, he has published over sixty stories and articles in publications such as Salon, The Southern Humanities Review, PANK, Hobart, and elsewhere. His work has been nominated for a handful of Pushcart's and The Million Writer's Award, was judged a finalist for the New American Fiction Prize by Lee K. Abbott and has been featured in Best of the Net and Wigleaf's Top 50 Fictions. His first book, *An End to All Things*, was released by Atticus Books in 2012. Split Lip Press will release his next two collections, *The Hook and the Haymaker* and *I Am the Oil of the Engine of the World*, in 2015 and 2016, respectively. In his spare time he serves as Editor-in-Chief of the literary magazine *BULL* and writes screenplays and covers politics. His website is at jysexton.com and he maintains a Twitter account at @jysexton.

Thank you for reading.
Please write a review of this book.
Reviews help others find newpulppress.com
And inspire us to keep bringing you
the best in crime noir.

http://www.newpulppress.com/

www.ingramcontent.com/pod-product-compliance
Lightning Source LLC
Chambersburg PA
CBHW070450260626
47161CB00004B/1265